HIDDEN SHIFTERS

HIDDEN SHIFTERS

DAVID DANN

DOOBIN PRESS

Doobin Press
Kalispell, Montana

Book cover and interior design by Monkey C Media
Cover and interior illustrations by Charlie Lively
Edited by Melissa Bloom
Author photo by Brad Golden
Illustrator photo by Kelly Cullen

First Edition
Printed in the United States of America

ISBNs:
979-8-9856168-0-4 (trade paperback)
979-8-9856168-1-1 (e-book)
979-8-9856168-2-8 (hardcover)

Library of Congress Control Number: 2022915480

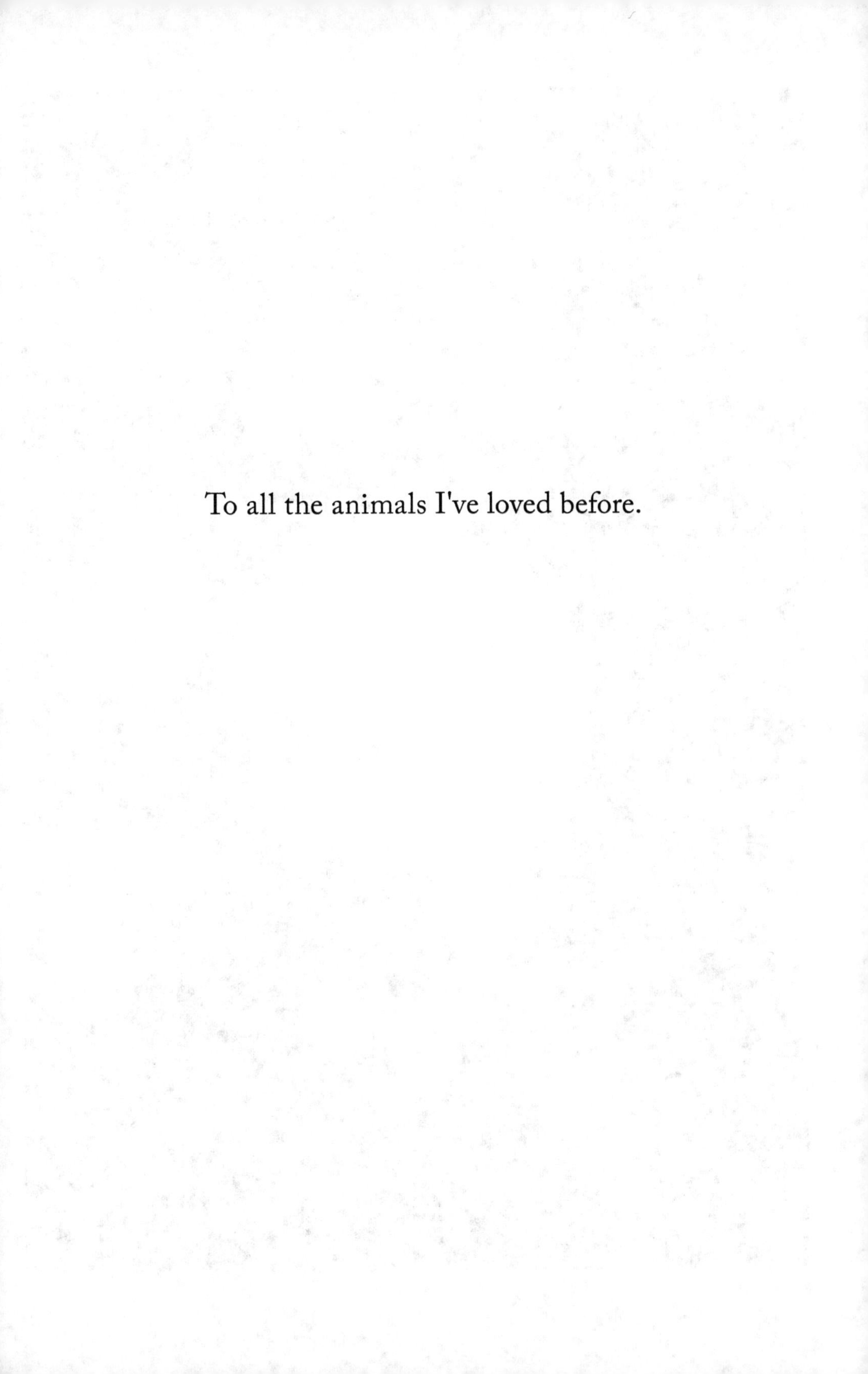

To all the animals I've loved before.

SOLAR SYSTEM A
A1
A2
A3
A4
A5
A6
A7
A8
A9
OUR STORY STARTS HERE

SOLAR SYSTEM B

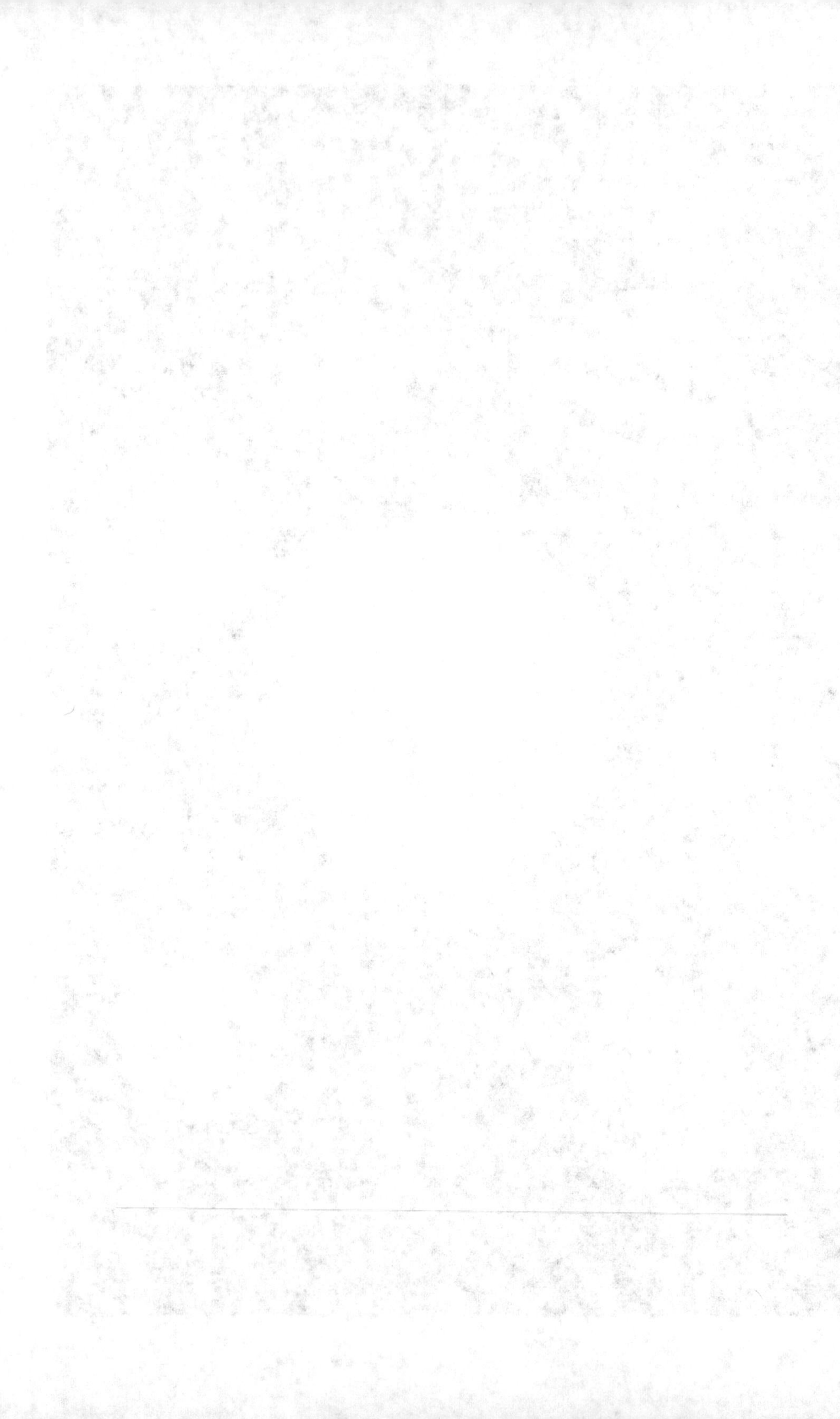

OF HUMANS, SHAPESHIFTERS, AND HYBRID CREATURES

SHAPESHIFTERS WEREN'T ALWAYS a threat on planet A7. A naturally docile species, their ability to transform into any shape evolved from their desire to blend in with the natural world of their home planet, A5. It's not surprising, then, that the human population of A7 welcomed them with open arms when they were forced to emigrate from their dying world. Their integration into society resulted in a new kind of being—a hybrid. Part human, part creature, hybrids eventually became the dominant species on the Earth-like planet. And though humans had long gone extinct, shapeshifters continued to call A7 home. That is, until the aliens invaded.

GUIDE TO HYBRID CREATURES

BEAR

Danger Rating: 8

Strengths: fast runner, keen sense of smell, lifting large loads, giving great hugs

Weaknesses: slow walker, near sighted doesn't know their own strength

BIRD

Danger Rating: 2

Strengths: Can fly, 180-degree line of sight, good at singing

Weaknesses: slow walker, poor hearing non-weight bearing, talkative

CAT

Danger Rating: 2

Strengths: Agile climber and jumper, can land upright from up to a height of 20 ft in the air, light-footed, quiet presence

Weaknesses: Water-adverse, take themselves too seriously

Dog
Danger Rating : 3
Strengths : fast runner, keen sense of smell and hyper sensitive hearing, agile swimmer
Weaknesses : Heavy-footed, messy eater, tends to get lonely

Dragon
Danger Rating : 10
Strengths : fire breathing, lifting large loads
Weaknesses : Heavy-footed, stubborn, tail can get in the way in small settings, requires a lot of food and water (can deplete resources)

Gorilla
Danger Rating : 8
Strengths : Climbing, weight lifting
Weaknesses : Lack of fine motor skills, clumsy

Horse

Danger Rating: 5

Strengths: fast runner, strong jaw and laugh, charming

Weaknesses: Think they're funnier than they are

Lizard

Danger Rating: 2

Strengths: super sight, hard to startle, slipping in and out of situations unnoticed, super chill

Weaknesses: Easy to forget about, weak grip, unmotivated

Monkey

Danger Rating: 4

Strengths: jumping and swinging long distances, climbing, grooming, singing

Weaknesses: Bananas

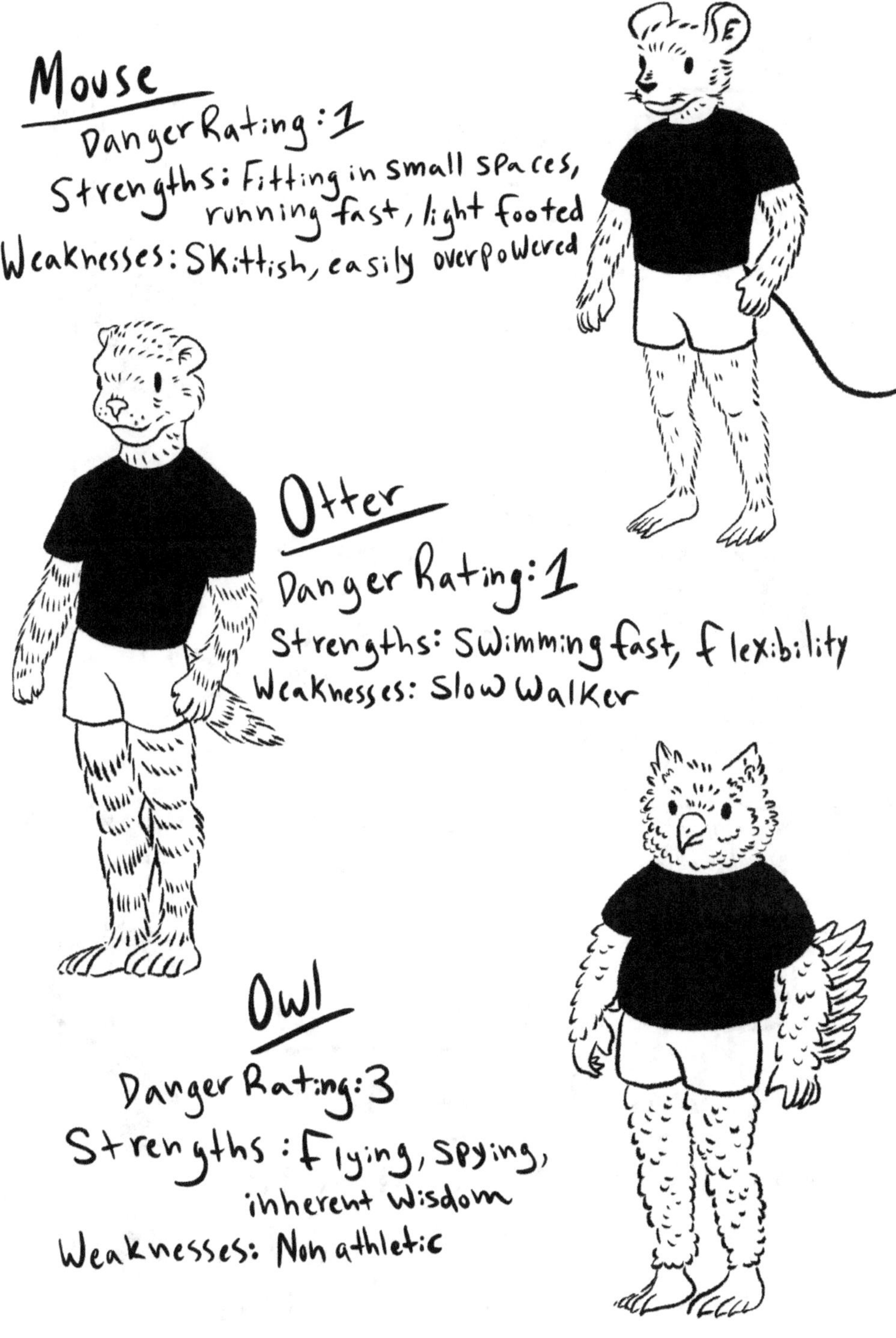

Mouse
Danger Rating: 1
Strengths: Fitting in small spaces, running fast, light footed
Weaknesses: Skittish, easily overpowered

Otter
Danger Rating: 1
Strengths: Swimming fast, flexibility
Weaknesses: Slow walker

Owl
Danger Rating: 3
Strengths: Flying, spying, inherent wisdom
Weaknesses: Non athletic

Rabbit

Danger Rating: 1

Strengths: sprinting, fitting into small areas, gardening

Weaknesses: High strung, easily startled

Raccoon

Danger Rating: 4

Strengths: smooth talker, acute hearing, observant

Weaknesses: Prone to scoliosis, untrustworthy

Shapeshifter

Danger Rating: 10+

Strengths: assumes strengths of hybrid creature it shifts into

Weaknesses: Insecure, untrusting

Sheep
Danger Rating :1
Strengths: Good listener, follows the rules
Weaknesses: Fragile limbs, Worrier

Tiger
Danger Rating: 9
Strengths: Agile, Sturdy, jumping, landing on feet, Sensing when someone is lying
Weaknesses: Inconsiderate, bad listener

Alien Anatomy

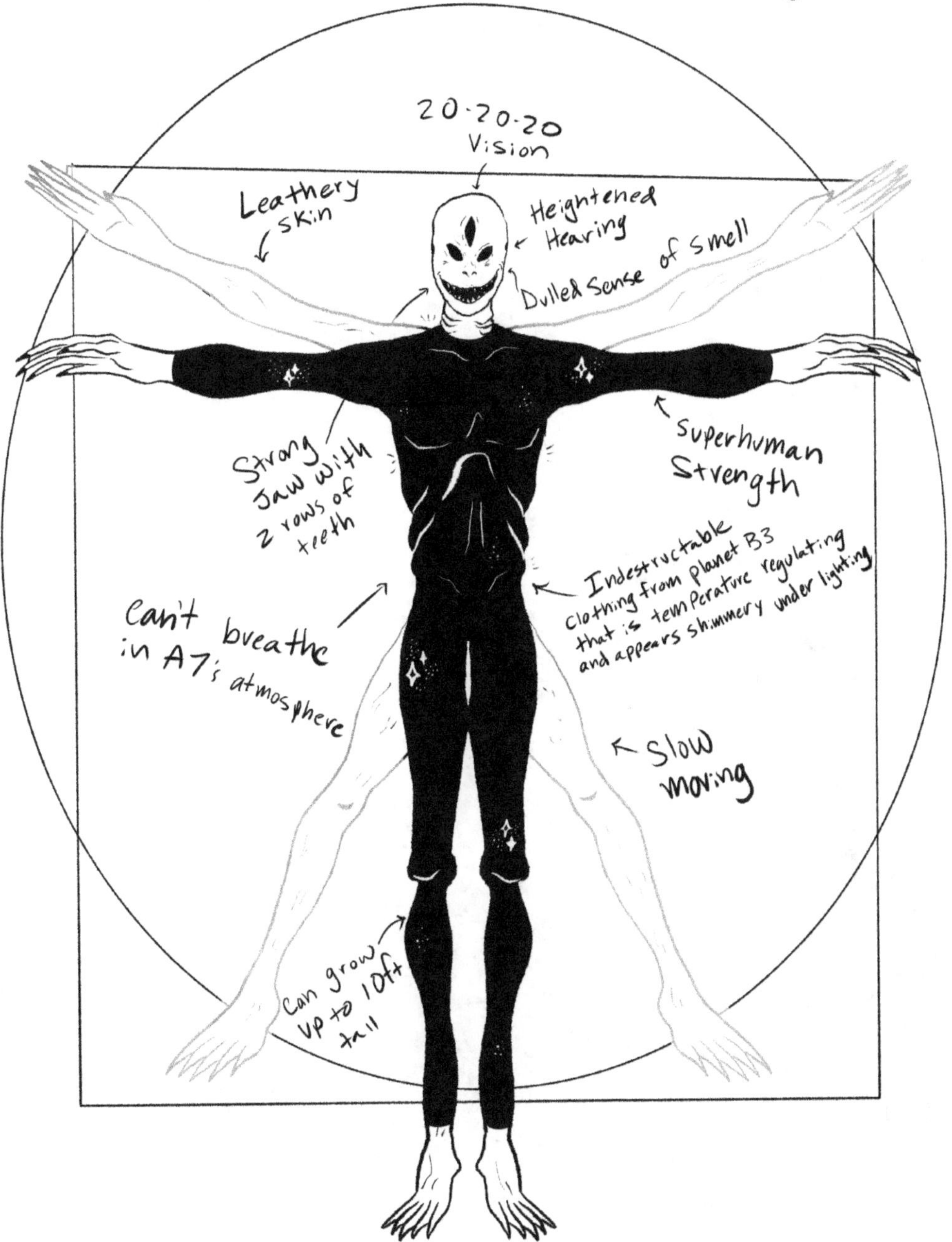

1

ADRIAN WALKER HAD only ever known to hide. He was too young to remember the day the aliens arrived, but he did remember the day they invaded. His parents shifted into sheep form and hid him in the closet until his abilities had developed enough for him to shift too. He thought once he transformed into a sheep, everything would go back to normal—they would move towns and start over as a sheep family that everyone could see was harmless. Instead, everything got worse.

The zoo that had been shut down since the humans went extinct was reopened. The aliens converted it into a prison for dangerous hybrids, and of course for the species they considered most dangerous of all: shapeshifters.

Adrian never planned on getting a job at the very place that threatened his existence, but he had learned quickly that on planet A7 the best place to hide was in plain sight. So when his best friend, Zeke, told him about the open janitor position five years ago, he applied.

Adrian started his shift like any other day, picking up trash, sweeping the floor, and cleaning up the cells, each of which held six prisoners. Like always, Adrian made sure to keep his eyes down—on his broom or his hooves—while he walked past the cells. Still, today he wasn't fast enough to dodge the clawed foot that suddenly appeared in front of him. His broom clattered loudly on the floor before he joined it with a thud. Wincing from the pain that shot through his arms, he pushed himself up quickly. He chanced a glance back at the dragon prisoner responsible, who wore a smug look. "Sorry, Sheeple," he said as if daring Adrian to start a fight.

Maintaining the hybrid appearance of a sheep should have offered him a low profile, but in prison, anyone outside the cells was watched enviously.

Adrian looked forward at his hooves again, doing his best to brush the dirt from his curly wool, and walked on to the next enclosure. This one was where the monkeys used to take sanctuary. Now it was overgrown with plant life that wound its way around the barred doors. Adrian began untangling the vines when he noticed the lock was loose. A bush rustled in the distance. There was a prisoner inside. And if he found out about the loose lock, there was a chance he would escape.

The warden needed to know.

Adrian gently set down his broom and backed away from the enclosure toward the warden's office at the front of the facility. He kept his head down passing the dragons again and the other hybrid creatures lining the pathway. He stepped up to the ticket booth that acted as the entrance to the office and rang the call bell. He waited. One minute. Two minutes. Rang again. But no one came.

"Hello?" Adrian called. "Warden Philly."

Adrian checked his watch. It was well into the workday. He nudged the door and it creaked open—unlocked. The warden always locked his door before he left for the day.

Adrian slowly entered the office. Papers were stacked so high on the desk that some had spilled onto the floor. The chair was facing the door as if the warden had just gotten up and walked away. A glass mug lay shattered beside the desk, a dark stain soaked into the carpet.

Adrian's heart pounded.

What the hell happened here?

Adrian walked out of the room and started his search for the warden, going area by area to find him. After scouring around for hours, he concluded that the warden was missing. A pit formed in his stomach as he walked to the parts and service room, which was located near the enclosure that had the loosened lock. Adrian opened the metal door and the automatic lights flickered on and then off. The room was very spacious with shelves that were ten feet tall. The shelves were also very organized, all thanks to him. Adrian went through the inventory list that was located twenty feet from the door. He found the lock he was looking for toward the middle of the parts and service room and headed down the closest aisle.

Suddenly he heard a metal pipe hit the ground around the corner. It rolled toward him as he approached. Two figures were backlit in the dim fluorescent glow. One was a horse-hybrid—the warden. The other was a humanoid robot he didn't recognize. Adrian got close enough to listen in on the conversation.

"Philly, you know that it is against the law to help the rebellion," said the robot.

"I told you, I don't know anything about them," said Philly.

"Your vitals indicate you're lying. Just when I was starting to like you," said the robot. It picked Philly up by the head with a metal hand that looked like it could crush it in an instant, and in one fell swoop, threw his body on the ground. As the blood oozed from his head, the shape began to morph. Within seconds, Warden Philly's horse body turned into a bear.

Adrian stumbled back and his hoof hit the metal pipe that had fallen earlier. The robot swiveled toward the noise and moved in Adrian's direction. Adrian got a good look at the robot's face, which was shaped like a wolf's head, made of a foreign metal that almost appeared to glow. His electronic eyes scanned ahead. Adrian ran to the door. The robot followed, running after him on a pair of sleek metal legs. Adrian knocked over a few shelves on his way to the door. He thrust it open, slipped through, and pressed himself against it to shut it, locking it in the process. A few seconds later there was a big metallic thud against the door. Adrian dove behind a bush, heart pounding. He waited for the robot to come barreling out of the door. But all was quiet.

After a few more moments, Adrian stood and walked zombie-like to the enclosure and fixed the lock. As he walked, he wondered if what he saw was a dream. *Was the warden really dead? Had he really shapeshifted right before he died? If so, did the aliens know? Who was that robot?*

All Adrian knew was that he didn't want to be involved in any of it. He took a deep breath while he replaced the lock. The actual process only took a few minutes, but Adrian stood there until the sun began to set. He made a beeline to the exit and inserted his card to be time-stamped.

A deep voice startled him. "Clocking out early?"

Adrian turned to find his best friend Zeke, who was head of security. Someone he could tell about what he saw. Someone who would do something about it. He stood there, mouth hanging open, unable to get the words out.

Zeke let out a chuckle from his scaly mouth, his lizard tongue flapping. He slapped Adrian on the shoulder with his tail. "Just kidding. It's only a few minutes to closing." He winked a beady eye.

Adrian gathered his mouth into a forced smile. "See you tomorrow," he managed.

■ ■ ■

Adrian brought his hoof to his apartment door and knocked: three times hard, two times soft, one more time hard. A series of clicks and snaps sounded from the other side. A sheep's face similar to his appeared as the door slowly creaked open. His girlfriend, Anna, stepped aside as he rushed in. He slammed the door shut, relocking each of the six different-style locks.

"Adrian, what's wrong?" Anna asked, transforming back into the tiger form he knew her as.

Adrian crossed the room and shut the blinds tighter than they already were. "Something happened today."

"What do you mean?"

"The warden is dead."

Anna's face went pale. "How do you know?"

"He was working for the rebellion. This robot thing killed him. Like he was an overripe watermelon. Just bam. Gone." Adrian accentuated his point by pounding one of his hooves into another.

Anna lowered onto the couch as she stared off into space. "You know what this means, don't you?"

"That we're in more danger than ever," he said.

She met his eyes. "It means the rebellion is working. We can have more freedom if we join them and win."

"My boss was killed for the cause and you call that working?"

"Yes."

"I saw him—transform. When he died. Did you know that happens to shifters?"

Anna nodded. "My parents did."

Adrian swallowed the lump in his throat, for once grateful that he hadn't been there to see his parents die the way Anna had twelve years ago. The door to their home beat down, her mom helping her into the ceiling vent while her dad attempted to fight the aliens, ten-year-old Anna watching the whole thing from above, helpless.

For Adrian it was different. For Adrian, his parents kissed him goodnight, told him they were going to the movies and they would be there when he woke up. Instead, Zeke's dad was at the door to tell him his parents were gone.

Adrian placed his hand over the watch on his wrist. The only thing he had left to remember his father. He had nothing to remember his mother, just memories that were fading by the year.

His throat constricted with the thought and he cleared it. "Look, Anna, I don't feel comfortable with you attending protests right now. We need to lay low."

"This is bigger than us, Adrian. If we don't help, the aliens win."

"This isn't a superhero movie; it's real life."

"Exactly. And our parents have left us a legacy to defend. You don't want justice for them?"

"What legacy? As far as I'm concerned they threw their lives away for the cause. Whatever the cause is."

Anna stood. "I won't sit by useless, hiding in here while you're hiding out there at your job."

"I'm not hiding—" Adrian's nostrils flared as he breathed out.

"I know, I know. You're keeping us safe." Anna drew out the words as if they were a public service announcement.

"I can't do this tonight." Adrian walked to the table, where two bowls of pasta were waiting, and sat down.

Anna opened her mouth and then closed it. She plopped down in the chair across from him, arms crossed.

She watched him eat, her bowl getting cold in front of her.

"I'm sorry about Philly," she said. "He was the only thing good about that prison."

Adrian nodded, putting down his fork. "It's going to be tough to replace him."

2

THE NEXT DAY at work, Adrian went straight to the parts and service room. He needed to be certain about what he saw. He needed to figure out why the warden had been killed. He punched the code into the keypad and unlatched the door. The room was dark. He turned on the overhead lights, which flickered ominously. Through the dim lighting, he examined the room. Everything was in its place—not a part missing or dirty. No blood, no dents in the shelving or walls, no sign of a struggle. Someone had cleaned up the mess. Or had there never been one to begin with? Had Adrian imagined the whole thing? Maybe the warden was back in his office right now, and he'd been worried for nothing.

Adrian spun, heading for the door. His chest hit a clunk of metal, sending a shock down his spine as he hit the ground.

It was the robot from yesterday. The one who had killed the warden.

Adrian's breath left him. He pressed off the floor, scooting back into a shelf. He was trapped.

"Janitor. What duty brings you here?"

Even though they were of similar height in his sheep form, the robot's build was simultaneously more slender and sturdy. His wolf head met a thick, tapered torso where Adrian assumed his central controls lived. His arms and legs were jointed. An image flashed in his head of those metal hands picking Warden Philly up by the head.

"Wh-who are you? *What* are you?" Adrian found himself stuttering.

"I am Caesar, AI companion to our leader."

Adrian knew who the leader was. The head of the alien clan, simply known as Jack. He had never met her face to face, only seen her at their rallies and prison inspections surrounded by a pack of guards.

Caesar continued. "You are janitor Adrian Walker, correct?"

Adrian contemplated lying but figured that wouldn't end well considering he was wearing his ID badge. "Yeah . . . ," he said.

"Leader would like to meet with you now."

"Now?"

"Yes, follow me."

Realizing this was an order, Adrian followed Caesar past the enclosures and the warden's office to an area of the prison he had never been before. He had seen it on the maps as "restricted area" and had been told to never ever clean there. Adrian knew it used to be the wide open space where giraffes and elephants could roam and assumed it was just an abandoned field now. But every once in a while he saw guards escorting prisoners that way.

As Caesar pushed aside some overgrown bushes, he saw what was hiding there: a honeycomb-shaped structure made of rough, dulled metal. It was tall, but not so tall that the trees couldn't hide it from a distance. Caesar extended his robot arm and at its end a cylindrical key appeared. He inserted it into one of the divots on the scratched surface. His arm twisted a full three hundred sixty degrees until suddenly a door appeared, recessing from the surface and sliding open.

Adrian caught his breath and followed Caesar into a small chamber.

"Commence decontamination," Caesar announced.

"Decontam—" before Adrian could get the word out, a hot gust of wind rushed over him and suspicious steam rose up from the ground that made his skin clam up. Adrian pinched his eyes shut and waited for the uncomfortable sensation to pass. Soon, the heat turned to ice-cold as the steam dissipated. Goosebumps prickled his skin, but before the cold was overbearing, that too passed. The temperature returned to normal and the door opposite where they entered opened.

"This way," Caesar said as if nothing had happened. But his metal body did look much shinier than before.

Now they were in a smaller chamber lined with suits hanging along the walls.

Caesar pulled one down. "According to my calculations, this suit will fit you nicely."

"Why do I need this?" Adrian asked.

"To breathe, of course," the robot said.

It was an oxygen suit. Adrian stepped his way into it and the robot helped him suit up.

The next door opened and they were in a large, circular space that led to several different hallways. All of them were identical and fear shot through Adrian as he realized he wouldn't be able to find his way out of there alone. Caesar led him through the center hallway and Adrian tried to count how many hallways there were to the one where they came from.

But the hallway didn't lead straight ahead. It veered right into the next hallway and zig-zagged like a maze—or a honeycomb. Adrian's nerves clenched his jaw tighter with each step. Where was this robot taking him?

Adrian did his best to glance in the rooms they passed. He noted labs with beakers and test tubes—items he knew the aliens had confiscated from the hybrids' laboratories and scientists. All of them were now shut down, run down. The only experiments and research happening were the ones the aliens approved of.

A loud bang drew his attention to the right. The whole wall shuddered as a face appeared in the closest window. It morphed from dragon snout to human nose to bird beak and back to human. A shapeshifter. Could it be the warden? But Adrian had seen him dead.

The prisoner's mouth formed the word, "Help!" but the sound was unable to reach the hallway.

"Goodness," Caesar said. He paused and punched the button on the wall. The lights above turned red. "That will be taken care of. Please, this way."

Adrian's legs suddenly felt like jelly. He wasn't sure he could take another step. Thankfully, the door ahead opened. Caesar turned back to him. "Our leader will see you now."

Adrian took a deep breath and picked up his left leg, then his right leg, then his left again. One excruciating step after the other, until he was inside.

The room was angular yet large. Strange found objects like bicycle wheels, corkscrews, and seashells decorated the shelves and walls like treasured trophies. A metal desk rose out of the center of the room. Behind it was the tallest alien Adrian had ever seen—and she was sitting down. She must have been nearly ten feet tall. Like all the aliens, her head was shaped like a potato, round and lumpy. Three eyes were inset in a triangle on her forehead and her mouth was broad across her whole face. Two holes appeared to stand in for ears on either side of her head and gills opened and closed on her leathery neck. She smiled to reveal shark-like teeth. The only pleasant thing about her was the long shimmery cloak draped over her body, grazing the floor. Adrian tried not to cringe as she spoke in a low, raspy voice.

"Adrian Walker. I am Jack. Deepest thanks for meeting me."

"Um, sure," he managed.

"Please." She gestured for him to sit so he did. "I won't keep you long. I wanted you to hear the news from me directly."

"What news?" he asked, though he was sure he knew.

"How well did you know Warden Philly?"

Adrian's heart sank. He knew his answer could determine what the most powerful alien on the planet thought of him. What she would do to him. "He was my superior . . . ," Adrian began. "I went to him for my orders. If I had questions. That's all."

Jack's middle eye seemed to bore into his forehead, as if she was reading his thoughts.

"So you weren't aware that he was a shapeshifter?"

"No," he said almost too quickly. He straightened in his seat. "No, I was not."

Jack got up, walked around the desk, and moved next to Adrian, towering over him. "Can you elaborate on that please?"

"Well, I'm just a janitor. No one tells me anything."

"Valued point but I expect better from you in the future now that you are the new warden."

"The new—what? Me, warden?" Adrian shook his head.

"You do understand that this kind of offer doesn't come around all the time."

Adrian opened and shut his mouth. The way she said, "offer" made him wonder what would happen if he refused.

"Do we have a problem?" she asked.

Adrian shook his head again, craning his neck to chance a glance at that otherworldly face.

"Then you may rise. I suspend you from your janitorial duties today. Go home and get some rest. Tomorrow you arrive at work as warden." She turned to the robot. "Caesar, you will take Adrian on a tour tomorrow for educational purposes."

"Yes, Leader."

She flicked her webbed hand. "That's settled. Caesar will escort you out."

Adrian stood as Caesar glided forward, robot arms outstretched. He jumped back as they jabbed his legs. "I can walk!" Adrian said and ran out with Caesar at his heels.

3

WHEN HE LEFT work, Adrian walked to the subway as fast as he could and chose an empty car. He couldn't believe he had been face to face with the alien leader. With any alien. He'd only ever seen them covered in protective gear that allowed them to breathe in A7's atmosphere. But Jack had been completely uncovered. He shivered at the thought of that face. Her skin, her eyes. Adrian gripped the subway car railing as he swayed from the motion of it turning. All he wanted to do was be inside his locked apartment with Anna. To tell her what happened. That he, of all people, had been promoted to warden. Why him? He still didn't understand it.

When he was finally at the door, Adrian commenced his secret knock. But no locks clicked behind the door. He tried again and pressed his ear to the door. Still nothing. He dared not say Anna's name. He fumbled in his pocket and retrieved his keys, inserting and turning each of the six into their respective locks.

The lights and TV were on when he entered. The blinds were drawn shut. But no Anna. Adrian's heart sank into his gut as he remembered their talk the night before. She had not listened. She was at the rebel rally.

Adrian moved to the closet, where he reached for a plain black T-shirt and jeans. A small box tumbled out of the shirt and onto the floor. The engagement ring he had bought a few months ago. He still hadn't asked her. It would be so simple: to pull it out one night and ask. But one night after the next just kept going by.

Adrian rolled the box back up in the black T-shirt, stuffing it in with his socks. He chose a gray shirt instead and changed out of his work clothes. He imagined a rabbit in his mind's eye. Familiar cramps overtook his body as the tufts of fuzzy wool from his sheep form smoothed into fluffy fur, his arms and legs shrinking by a few inches. His stomach gave a final lurch and he knew the transformation was complete. Even though a sheep was the least intimidating form, he couldn't chance anyone from the prison recognizing him. No one would care about a rabbit.

Adrian then headed out the door and proceeded to the rally. When he arrived, he could see it was packed. He headed toward the building, brushing past a family of actual rabbits. He brushed his ears down self-consciously as he surveyed the area, full of hybrids and vendors. Feeling overwhelmed, Adrian continued his search for Anna. Various merchants vied for his attention, but one, in particular, stepped into his path.

"Oy buddy, that's a nice watch," the raccoon said. "I can offer you a pretty penny for it."

Adrian realized the man owned a pawn shop. He crossed his arms, tucking the watch under his elbow. "Oh, this is a family heirloom. I'm not interested in selling."

Now the man clawed at his arm. "Name your price. Any price."

Adrian's heart skipped as the man's grip tightened. "I'm sorry. This watch is priceless. It's all I have left from my parents."

There was something knowing in the raccoon's face. "Is that so." Hunger flashed behind his eyes. "Ever heard of Madame Universe?"

"Yeah, I guess. It's just a legend."

The man took a step closer to Adrian. "Some say she has the power to turn back time. To crown kings and queens, make empires fall. To rechart the course of history in favor of the one who finds her."

"So?" Adrian tried to take a step back, but a display sign was in his way.

"Others say the rebellion made contact with her years ago. That she is the key to ending the tyranny of the aliens."

Adrian's heart jumped and he looked around to see who heard. "You can't say that kind of thing."

The man narrowed his eyes, focusing in on Adrian as if he had X-ray vision. "Tell me, son. Who were your parents?"

Adrian opened and shut his mouth, realizing if he said his parents' names, this man would know who—and what—he was.

Suddenly an urgent voice aired over the crowd. "Rebels have infiltrated the building. Please remain calm and walk in an orderly fashion to the exit."

The clutch on Adrian's arm loosened. The raccoon had disappeared.

Anna, Adrian thought. He rushed toward the building. If she was in there, he had to get to her before the aliens did. But her voice came from the opposite direction. "Let me go!"

Adrian turned and darted toward her struggling voice. A cat was being dragged by two masked alien guards. Her usual protest form was a rabbit, but he glimpsed the horseshoe-shaped scar on her neck. It was her. Adrian fought against the crowd to get closer. They were almost to their vehicle. He panicked and yelled, "Anna!"

Anna's head snapped toward his voice. "Adrian?"

Before he could get to her, something heavy collided with the back of his head. Everything went black.

How Adrian and Anna met...
Their Parents were best friends.
They played together all the time.
Until the day Adrians parents didn't come home.
He learned they were killed during a mission for the resistance.
And was taken in by his best friend Zeke's family.
Anna and Adrian still played.

Until the day Anna's parents were also killed by the aliens.
Anna was sent to a foster home.
And then another.
And then another.
Anna and Adrian no longer played.

10 years later...
Anna and Adrian ran into eachother.

It was love at first sight
(or second sight.)

ADRIAN'S EYES FLUTTERED open, the gray ceiling going in and out of focus. He lifted his head and winced as a throbbing pain shot down his neck. Then he remembered. The rally and Anna, the aliens taking her. And—then what? He rolled to his side and was met with a series of vertical bars. Past them was just another wall. Panic coursed through him—had the aliens caught him too? Had he been captured and thrown in the jail he was supposed to be running?

Adrian struggled to his feet and examined the cell. It was small, plain, unlike the rooms he had seen on the way to meet Jack. And nothing like the cells he walked past daily to clean at the zoo. This was a different kind of jail. One he had never seen before.

Adrian peered through the bars, craning his neck to see down the barren tunnel. "Hello?"

The cement walls absorbed his voice. He tried again, shaking the bars as he yelled. "Is anyone there? Hello!"

He strained to listen to the sounds around him. But all he heard was his own breath and a slight buzzing from the single light bulb overhead.

Adrian paced, scanning the cell. The bars were thinner than the ones at the prison, but perhaps the locks were the same. He moved to the side of the cell and felt around the corner. His hand ran over a large keyhole. His heart rose. Piece of cake.

Adrian rested his index finger over the keyhole and shut his eyes. He visualized the key turning in the lock. His finger cramped and incrementally slid into the keyhole. Adrian rotated his wrist and there was a click. He removed his finger and a gap appeared between the cell bars and the wall. Adrian pushed it open. He'd done it. He was free.

Adrian looked left down the hallway into an empty expanse. Then he looked right. Two gorilla guards cocked their guns; between them stood a woman—a dog—with her arms folded over her chest. "I'm glad I caught you before you left," she said.

Adrian looked down at his finger, still in the shape of a key, and hid it behind his back. Did she see it? Did she know what he was? No, she couldn't.

Adrian took a step back. "Who are you?"

"You almost got yourself captured there," she said. "If it wasn't for me, you'd be under an alien magnifying glass right now."

Adrian brought his hand to the back of his head.

The woman winced in commiseration. "Sorry about that. You didn't give me much choice."

"Where's Anna? Where am I?"

"Anna knew the dangers going into the rally."

"You let them take her!" Adrian lunged for the woman, but the guards caught him instead. He struggled in their grasp. "I almost had her."

"You have no idea what you're in possession of, do you?"

Adrian stopped struggling and rested a hand over his father's watch as he remembered the merchant's obsession with it. "I don't have anything," he said.

The woman eyed his wrist for longer than Adrian was comfortable with and then walked closer to him. "Did you know about your girlfriend's allegiance to the rebel cause?"

"Allegiance? She attended some rallies. That's all."

The woman signaled to the guards to hang back and she put a paw on Adrian's shoulder. It was a stronger grip than he imagined would come from a dog. There was something about this woman. Something off.

"You work at the prison," she said. "A janitor." There was no question in her voice.

Adrian couldn't believe this stranger knew so much about him. Anna must have told her everything. "Why?" was all he could manage.

"Anna made it clear from the beginning that she didn't want you to be a part of this. That she wanted to protect you, but the aliens are growing stronger."

"Protect me? How is this protecting me?"

"The rebel cause is also growing stronger. We have more allies than ever. More recruits by the day. But our technology is no match for the aliens. No matter how big our forces are, it won't be enough if our weapons can't compare. What we need is an inside man."

Adrian's eyes widened. She couldn't be serious.

She continued. "Someone who has access to their tools, their weapons. Someone who can slip in and out of situations. Someone who has reason to be in a supply closet. In the aliens' spaces. Someone who can go undetected."

"You've got me all wrong," he said.

"Do you know what the aliens do to shapeshifters when they're caught?"

The image of the shapeshifter pounding on the door on the way to Jack's office flashed in Adrian's mind. How much did this woman know? "Why would I care about shapeshifters?" Adrian lied.

The woman gave him a knowing look. "You can help us get Anna back."

Adrian's watch beeped, making him jump. He looked at the time on his wrist. "I'm going to be late for work."

"I'll have my guards escort you."

"No, I can find my own way."

The woman nodded and gestured for him to follow. She walked him down a series of tunnels to a metal door. She pressed the door open and waited for him to walk through. "If I was you, I wouldn't take that off." Her eyes flicked to his watch and then back to his face. "We'll be in touch."

The door shut between them and Adrian stood dumbstruck for a moment before ducking behind the dumpster and shifting back into sheep form.

WHILE ON HIS way to work, Adrian couldn't stop thinking about what just happened to him. Could Anna be all that?

It didn't really matter. All that mattered was that Adrian find her and save her from whatever the aliens had in store.

Adrian clocked in and was met by Zeke.

"Adrian, you'll never believe the rumors floating around. They're saying you're the new warden. How crazy is that?"

Great. In the span of twenty-four hours, I went from invisible to having rumors spread about me, Adrian thought.

He looked left and right, then pulled Zeke into an empty hallway. "They aren't rumors."

Zeke's jaw dropped. "Oh my gosh! You're kidding! My bestie is the Big Cheese of the place? No way. Can I touch you? I'm in the presence of greatness."

Zeke poked Adrian's arm. "You feel different," he said.

Adrian slapped his finger away. "You've never physically touched me before!"

Zeke straightened. "Right. So. What's your first order, boss?"

Adrian pulled him further down the hallway and lowered his voice. "I need a favor."

"At your service."

"I need you to keep your eyes peeled for Anna. If you see her at all today, come find me immediately."

"Hold on, wait. Why would Anna be here at the jail? You guys have a lunch date or something?"

Adrian braced Zeke, looking into his darting eyes. "If you see Anna, *anywhere*, at any point today, just come find me, okay?"

"Janitor."

Adrian jumped at the robotic voice. He turned to find Caesar not a foot behind him.

"It is time for your induction ceremony," Caesar said. "Please follow me."

Adrian glanced back at Zeke and gestured for him to come too.

They followed Caesar through the west side of the prison to the second greenhouse. Every single staff member was packed inside, along with several figures wearing hazmat suits—aliens. Adrian wondered if Jack would be there. His heart began to pound.

"Wait here," Caesar told Adrian and Zeke. Caesar left, disappearing behind a curtain of vines where everyone was facing. A few minutes later, Caesar reappeared, his voice projecting over the room. "Greetings aliens and hybrids. Boys and girls and everything in between. I introduce you to the one and only Jack."

The aliens began to clap loudly. Adrian and Zeke exchanged a look and slowly brought their hands together once.

Jack emerged from the vines in her suit and said, "Thank you all for coming here today. I am extremely proud of the progress our races have made together in our efforts to coexist peacefully on this planet. This facility and many others like it are ensuring the safety of our law-abiding citizens. As some of you may have noticed, Warden Philly is missing among us. It turns out he was not abiding by our laws. And so he has been removed as warden. But we have a very special guest here." Jack's eyes searched the audience and Adrian knew they would land on him. She extended her arm in his direction and the crowd clapped. "Adrian Walker, please come up." Adrian's stomach flip-flopped as he began to walk to where Jack stood.

Jack continued talking. "While we wait for Adrian I'd like to introduce you to your new janitor. Our engineers have been working on it for quite some time."

A stout robot whizzed past Adrian on conveyor belt wheels. Once it stopped beside Jack, Adrian could take in its unusual design. It had four arms, each a different cleaning tool: mop, vacuum, broom, and dustpan. Its head was a wide cylinder with a screen for eyes and a small camera mounted above it.

Adrian couldn't help but feel embarrassed by this representation of his janitorial role. For the first time, he actually felt pride in his old job and the more nuanced duties he performed. But it didn't matter. He had no choice here.

When Adrian reached Jack, she dismissed the robot and faced him. "Adrian, do you accept all duties and responsibilities of the position of warden?" Adrian hesitated, looking over at Zeke, who gave him a thumbs up. Adrian looked back at Jack and said, "Yes, I accept." The crowd applauded.

"There you have it. Thank you all for taking the time out of your day to be here. If you have any questions or concerns, Adrian is here for you."

Before Adrian knew what was happening, Jack was gone and a swarm of aliens and hybrids surrounded him, all talking at once.

"Congratulations," some were saying.

"I need to schedule a meeting to discuss . . . ," others cried.

"One at a time," Adrian said, but his voice came out as a squeak. He had never needed to speak to more than one person before.

"Okay," Zeke's voice boomed as his friend stepped beside him. "The warden has time-sensitive business to attend to. But he'd be happy to address your grievances if you leave a memo in his mailbox." Zeke tugged on Adrian's arm, pulling him through the crowd and out of the greenhouse.

"Holy cheese balls!" Zeke said. "That was crazy."

"Thanks for getting me out of there," Adrian said.

"Warden!" Caesar appeared behind them. "I will now give you a tour."

Adrian hesitated, wanting nothing more than to be invisible again so he could look for Anna. "That's okay, Caesar—"

"I must follow orders," Caesar bellowed. "Back to work, security."

"Yes, sir." Zeke saluted and hung back, shrugging at Adrian.

Adrian let Caesar go ahead of him and mouthed to Zeke, "Find Anna."

Zeke nodded and took off in the other direction.

Adrian followed the robot to the entrance of the jail.

"Let the tour commence," Caesar said.

"Really, Caesar, I already know—"

"On your left, you'll find the log booth. Here you will clock in and out daily promptly at 0900 and 1700 hours."

"I know that—"

"And on your right. . . ."

Caesar would not let Adrian get a word in edgewise. Adrian endured an hour of retracing every inch of the prison he knew like the back of his hoof.

As they approached his office, his shoulders slumped. Finally, he could get some time alone to process and make a plan for finding Anna.

Caesar stopped before the warden's office and turned to face him. "Now we will tour the alien compound."

Adrian's heart leapt. If Anna was truly being held prisoner, maybe he would find her on the tour.

Adrian followed Caesar as they went through the steps like the first time he met with Jack. Into the decontamination room, then the chamber with the oxygen suit, then into the open space.

Aliens passed through the area, throwing him curious glances.

"This way," Caesar says.

He led Adrian through the high-domed lobby area, where there was now an assortment of bright colorful lights moving on the other side of the transparent ceiling. They moved slowly, almost as if pulsing. It was mesmerizing.

"Hey, Caesar, those weren't there last time I was here."

"Negative, warden. The energy source never stays in the same place for long."

The energy source. Adrian knew the aliens had harnessed something from their old planet to sustain them. But tiny balls of moving light?

"How do they work?"

"Think of them like solar panels for your sun. They have a charge that sustains the species. The movement through the craft allows it to recharge on its own."

"Huh." Adrian could have stayed there all day watching the lights, but Caesar nudged him along, through a maze of hallways and doors, though he did not let Adrian see into any of the rooms.

Before he knew it they were back at the entrance.

"Tour complete," Caesar announced.

Adrian's insides felt heavy as the reality sunk in: Anna was not there. She was not anywhere in the prison. What if they had decided not to hold her prisoner, but worse? What if they decided to silence her for good?

Caesar turned to face Adrian. "Fearless Leader will see you now."

"What?" Adrian reeled. He could not imagine standing in front of Jack right now, putting on a happy face to the most powerful alien on the planet.

Adrian's feet were heavy as he followed Caesar to Jack's office. He glanced at the window where he'd seen the helpless shapeshifter banging, but the room was empty. Everything was quiet.

The door to Jack's office opened before Adrian and Caesar had reached it, like the first time. It seemed Jack was always a step ahead of everyone.

This time, Caesar stopped beside the door. Adrian stepped across the threshold into the office. There Jack sat behind her desk and beside her someone else in an oxygen suit stooped, clearing a tray of food.

"Ah, Adrian. I trust your tour went well."

The stooping figure's head raised toward him. And even though she was in an oxygen suit, he could still see the familiar horseshoe-shaped scar on her neck. He knew without a doubt: it was Anna.

How the Aliens Invaded A7

The aliens hail from Solar System B, on a Planet called B3.

Over many years, their technological advancements depleted their Planet's vital resources.

They harnessed the last bit of energy they could and set off to find a new home.

An equal distance from the Sun, they settled on Planet A7 in Solar System A.

They landed with good intentions and were met with A7 Council's hospitality.
OUCH
But there were Problems...
Then one day something terrible happened.
PRISON
And the aliens stopped playing nice.

ADRIAN'S BREATH LEFT him. He couldn't take his eyes off Anna. But she kept her head down as she passed him with the tray.

"Adrian." Jack was looking at him expectantly. She had asked him a question, hadn't she?

"Yes," he managed. He wanted to follow Anna. To take her hand and run out of the building, out of the prison, and escape. Like he'd wanted to.

"I wanted to make certain you were familiar with the entire layout of the prison. As the janitor, you were responsible for only some areas and now you are responsible for all of them. Your job was to keep everything clean and now it's to keep everyone in line. To report back to me if anything goes awry."

Adrian nodded. "Yes, ma'am."

He felt a presence reenter the room and Anna's arm grazed his as she passed him again and took her place next to Jack.

He couldn't keep his eyes off her. Why wasn't she looking at him?

"I see you've noticed my new assistant. This is Fiona Whiskers. Fiona, this is Adrian Walker."

Finally, Anna looked him in the eyes. "Hello," she said softly.

Adrian opened his mouth but nothing came out. He was certain it was Anna, but she had even changed her voice.

"H-hi," he finally said. His throat was getting drier by the minute.

"Do you have any questions?" Jack asked.

Did he have any questions? He had so many he wasn't even sure which one to start with. How did Anna become Jack's assistant when she should have been imprisoned like everyone else? Did Jack know who she really was? Was this all a big prank being played on him?

Instead, Adrian shook his head.

"Good. Caesar will escort you back to your office then."

Adrian couldn't move. He wanted to run to Anna. To make up an excuse to bring her with him. But Caesar had come to his side and his robot arm was poking his leg. "This way," Caesar said.

The second Adrian was out the door, it slammed shut.

He had been so worried Anna was being experimented on. Imprisoned. Killed. But this? This was even worse. How would he ever get to her again with her right under Jack's thumb?

FOR THE REST of the day in his office, the only thought Adrian could think was helping Anna. As soon as the clock struck five, he bolted for the exit.

As Adrian approached, Zeke looked up from his post expectantly.

Adrian nodded and Zeke's eyes widened. "You found—the thing you lost earlier in the . . . ?" He cleared his throat.

Adrian covered quickly. "Yeah, I found my—watch. But I can't get it back. It's stuck in the gutter. I need your help getting it back."

"Wait, you dropped your watch? I thought you lost—oooh." Zeke punched his card and walked with Adrian outside the prison. "So how can I help?"

Adrian smiled at the passing guard who was eyeing him. "Have a good night."

"You too, warden," the bird squawked.

He turned back to Zeke. "You want to come over tonight? Watch some TV? I'll make nachos."

"Well, sure, but what about the watch?"

Adrian pulled him further from the prison's exit. "We can talk about the watch tonight."

"Okay, I see how this is going. Got it, boss." He winked. "See you later."

Adrian watched Zeke wander toward his car. Then he turned around, taking in the expansive prison, backlit by the setting sun. He'd never thought about the prisoners inside until now. Had never thought about their stories, about why they were there. He only thought about his life, his job, his girlfriend. About staying outside the bars. And now the most important person in the world to him was trapped inside.

He could trust Zeke, he knew he could. But if he really wanted help, he needed to find the people Anna trusted. The reason she was taken prisoner in the first place.

■ ■ ■

Adrian got off at his usual subway stop, sticking as close to his normal route home as possible, and then cut back through town until he found the door where the rebel had let him out. He crouched behind the dumpster where he shifted before going to work and shifted back into the rabbit form he took for the rally. Then he walked back to the door and banged with all his might, over and over, until finally someone opened it.

Before he knew what was happening, the figure pulled him inside and shut the door. Adrian fell to his knees, planting his paws to look up at whoever it was. This time it wasn't the woman from before. A dragon towered over him, his hunched back grazing the ceiling of the tunnel. His massive tail swung from one wall to the other, thick scales catching the artificial light.

Adrian threw his arms above his head. "Please don't hurt me. I was here earlier. I spoke to uh—uh, she was a dog. She was your leader. She—she knows about my girlfriend, Anna. Anna was taken. She . . ."

"Relax. I know who you are. Welcome back." The dragon gave his leg a light kick. "The name's Blood Cry." His voice was higher than

Adrian had expected from his menacing appearance. Not so much threatening as smooth.

Adrian stood and brushed off his knees. "Blood Cry. Is that a nickname or . . . ?"

Blood Cry glanced back as he headed down the tunnel. "We were taking bets for how long it would take you to come back."

Adrian started after him. "You knew I'd come back?"

"Me? Nah, I thought you'd attempt some half-baked rescue mission for Anna and get captured within a day."

Adrian's cheeks flushed as he thought of the day's events, enlisting Zeke's help over nachos.

"Lola, on the other hand," Blood Cry continued. "She was sure you just needed a little time to process."

"Lola?"

Blood Cry clipped his voice so it sounded not unlike Caesar's robotic drone. "Our Fearless Leader."

Adrian thought of the mysterious dog who'd met him at his cell, who seemed to know so much more than she was letting on. She had to be his key to getting Anna back.

"I want to see her," Adrian said.

"Soon enough." Blood Cry kept walking, turning down another tunnel, this one sloping downward.

Adrian's feet slipped as the incline grew steeper. "Where are you taking me?"

This time Blood Cry didn't answer. He halted at the tunnel's outlet. Adrian stepped beside him. "Welcome to the resistance."

Adrian looked out into a vast open space. The tunnel walls extended into an expansive cave, stalactites and stalagmites jutting from every direction. In between the rock formations below were tents and carts of all kinds. Clotheslines draped from one stalagmite to another. Cardboard and wood overlapped and organized to form roofs.

And between the makeshift dwellings, hybrids bustled along cleared pathways. It was an entire town, right under their feet.

"Th—there are so many of them."

"It's an ongoing development. We have two rules. One—never tell anyone about us. And two—never turn anyone away."

Adrian continued to take in the colorful town and tried to count the number of people below. One question nagged at him. "How did Anna find you?"

"Let's keep moving."

Blood Cry led him down a pathway carved into the cave walls. Down and down they went, winding back and forth until they were finally at eye level with the town.

"I was one of the first down here. When the aliens started targeting dragons, gorillas, and bears. At first we thought we could fight them off. But you know how that turned out, don't you?"

Adrian thought of the prison population. There were a lot of dragons.

Blood Cry continued as they walked down the closest pathway, crowded with hybrids of all kinds and ages bustling about their dwellings. "It was Lola who found this place. She learned the sewage systems from her dad, who worked for the city's department of sewage and water. When the raids increased, she started taking families down the tunnels, setting them up, and bringing them food. It took a while to get this place up and running. But now we have running water, vertical gardens—the works to be self-sustaining."

A few young hybrids shot past them, laughing. Blood Cry pushed Adrian out of their path. "Good thing too, since Lola's now in hiding."

"So why fight?" Adrian asked. "All these protests and resistance rallies. You guys are safe down here. You could stay down here forever."

Blood Cry waited to reply until they were past the crowd. "Safe for now. And what about all my family members rotting in prison? What about those who weren't lucky enough to get down here? The aliens will find out about us one day. You can be sure of that."

"So why even try? What's the point?"

"We're biding our time. Training. Preparing for war."

"You think you can fight the aliens? And win?"

"You know that old saying—If you put a lobster in a boiling pot of water, it knows it's done for. But put that lobster in a cold pot of water and turn on the stove, the lobster doesn't even know it's boiling until it's too late."

"These are aliens we're talking about. Lots of aliens."

"Aliens who, as of now, can't breathe in our environment without masks."

"I've met Jack. They're too smart. They're going to know they're boiling faster than you can boil them."

Blood Cry pulled him into a corner. "Wait. You've met Jack?"

The blood drained from Adrian's face as he suddenly realized what he had just revealed.

"Only the warden gets to meet . . ." Blood Cry's eyes widened as he trailed off. He grabbed Adrian's arm and led him forward.

They wove in and out of more dwellings, passing vertical gardens constructed from PVC pipes and organized stacks of non-perishable foods like canned goods and freeze-dried snacks. Blood Cry made sure to smile or nod at each hybrid they passed, all of whom eyed Adrian with either suspicion or curiosity from their hammocks and lawn chairs. Adrian tried not to make eye contact and gathered that being associated with Blood Cry meant you had done something wrong or something was wrong in general. His heart pounded as he thought of where and what the dragon was leading him into.

After a while they stopped seeing anyone at all. It seemed they had reached the end of their town. They took a left, entering a huge sewer pipe, and eventually stopped at a pile of garbage bags. Blood Cry crouched next to the pile and moved a couple of the bags, revealing a lever. It screeched as he pulled it down. The cement wall next to the pile started to move and create a doorway. Blood Cry herded Adrian across the threshold, then repositioned the bags back to their places and shut the door.

The room they were now in was bright and warm. Blueprints lined the cement walls. A colorful rug covered the concrete floor. On top of it was a salvaged wooden table, pieced together from three different styles and types of wood.

Blood Cry stood at attention, nodding at the group of hybrids around the table who were all staring at them. Lola sat at the head, her hands pinning open a large map. Adrian couldn't make out what was on it.

Lola's eyebrows rose as she looked from Blood Cry to Adrian.

Blood Cry straightened. "Pardon the interruption, Lola. But I have pressing news."

Lola let the map go and it rolled back up. "Join us, then."

She sat and gestured to the empty seats closest to them.

All eyes remained on Adrian as they sat. His mind spun as he realized Blood Cry was about to tell everyone he was the new warden. He thought of Warden Philly, his mangled body in the supply closet. The repercussions of being in the rebellion. He knew without a doubt he did not want to meet the same fate.

Blood Cry glanced at Adrian and opened his mouth to tell his secret.

Adrian beat him to the punch. "I found Anna."

Something flickered in Lola's eyes, but her expression did not change. "Did you?"

"Jack's got her. She's basically her slave. It's only a matter of time before they find out she's a sha—" He stopped himself. Did all of them know Anna was a shapeshifter?

"I can assure you that everyone here is acting on Anna's best interests. There's nothing to worry about."

One of the generals cleared his throat. "How do you know that Anna's okay?"

"I saw her. She's being drugged or something. Barely looked at me. Jack said she's her new assistant. She's being forced to do anything Jack wants."

The men and women around the table exchanged disconcerting looks.

"We have to rescue her. That's why I came back. To tell you what I found out."

Lola folded her arms across her chest. "And we appreciate that very much, Adrian. But as I said, we have it under control. Unless you are here for another reason," she glanced at Blood Cry, "I'm going to have to ask you to please leave us to our business."

Blood Cry stood before Adrian could stop him. "He's the new warden."

Adrian's stomach clenched. Everyone at the table gasped and began muttering to one another.

Lola held up her hands. "Please."

They all looked to her.

"Thank you, Blood Cry." She turned her attention to Adrian.

His cheeks grew hot. What were they going to do to him now?

"Generals, let's reconvene at 0600 hours tomorrow."

Before the generals could react, Lola walked over to Adrian and Blood Cry. "Thank you, Blood Cry. You can go back to your watch now."

Blood Cry nodded and went back through the cement door.

Lola put her hand on Adrian's shoulder. "Are you hungry? I was just about to have dinner."

How the Resistance Was Born

After the accident that left an alien dead, the shapeshifter involved was forced to run.

His daughter, Lola, had a favorite cave near their house where she played and explored. There her father hid.

Unable to find him, the aliens started rounding up any threatening hybrid they set eyes on.

So Lola did something no other little girl would have done. She began going to her friends and neighbors and offering to hide those who would be taken to prison.

With each passing day, more and more hybrids gathered in caves, until they began to have a working society.
Then non-threatening animals began to be rounded up.
PRISON
Those in hiding decided it was time to act. When the day came, they would be ready to fight.

8

WHEN LOLA SAID dinner, Adrian assumed they would be going back to her office and be served as Jack was. Instead, he found himself behind her in line at the communal cafeteria.

There were hybrids of all sorts: dragons, dogs, gorillas, bears, cats, even an otter. It wasn't just the hybrids in danger of being imprisoned. Adrian wondered why the others were here, hiding in the dark when they could be living a perfectly good life above.

Lola handed him a plate. "Hope you like lasagna."

"I do." Adrian held his plate up to the cook—it was the raccoon who had tried to buy his watch. "It's you," he said.

"So it is." The raccoon glopped a pile of flat noodles and tomato sauce onto the plate. His eyes flicked to Adrian's wrist and his father's watch. "My offer still stands."

"No thanks." Adrian retracted his arms and turned to Lola, bringing the plate closer to examine the meatless and cheese-less dish.

"You've got to use your imagination," Lola said. "We work with what we can get down here." She led him to a table in the middle of the cafeteria, filled with hybrids. She plopped down next to a gorilla, then gestured in front of her where two bears were happily consuming their glop.

Adrian hesitated. This was where they were meeting? How was he supposed to talk about Anna?

The bears noticed his hesitation and self-consciously slid over to either side. Realizing he had no choice, Adrian stepped over the bench and squeezed between them.

Lola picked up her fork. "Corky and Coco, meet Adrian."

The bears on either side of him nodded their heads and said, "Nice to meet you," in unison. Up close he could see they were identical down to their pointy noses.

"Adrian is Anna's boyfriend. He's visiting."

The twins' eyes widened. "We love Anna," they said. "She's so brave."

"Wait—you know her?" Adrian glanced up and down the table. "You all know her?"

All at once, the hybrids at the table spoke over one another, Anna's name emitting from all of their lips.

Adrian's chest tightened. Anna had really been down here, working with the rebels. No wonder she was Jack's slave.

"Anna helped get Corky, Coco, and their mother down here," Lola said.

The twins nodded. Corky—or maybe Coco—spoke. "The aliens came for all of us. Our dad made us hide under the stairs. He said not to come out until we heard three hard knocks, two soft knocks, and one more hard knock."

The other twin added, "It was Anna. She led us to the closest secret entrance and we've been down here ever since."

Adrian felt as if the room were caving in on him. She had used their secret knock. The knock they had come up with to tell each other the coast was clear. That it was safe to come home.

"Hey, that's the knock she used with me too," the gorilla beside Lola said.

Adrian's stomach lurched. He shot up from the table and ran. He realized he had no idea where to go. How to get out. Where he was.

He found what he hoped was a trashcan and threw up.

A hand rested lightly on his lower back. Before he knew what was happening, the hand was guiding him gently yet firmly out of the cafeteria. Looking down, he recognized Lola's white-brown ombre fur. She guided him down a dim hallway and into a room.

"Why don't you lie down for a minute, huh?" Adrian heard her voice as if it was far away. He found himself horizontal suddenly, on an olive couch that by the looks of it used to be forest green. He did feel better lying down.

A glass of water hovered above him. "Drink this."

Adrian curled his torso and accepted the glass, slowly sipping its edge. She was being so nice to him—almost too nice.

"It wasn't my intention to upset you," Lola said. "But I need to show you something else and it may shock you."

Adrian pushed himself onto his elbows and managed to sit. What more was there that he didn't know about?

Lola turned on a large monitor on the far wall. There was Anna in the cafeteria Adrian had just come from. Anna as a sheep—her go-to shape—standing in front of a crowd. She cowered, curling up into a woolen ball. Then suddenly her body shifted, wool transforming into soft fur and she sprung up in rabbit form. She bounced onto a nearby table and jumped again, shifting in mid-air to a monkey. Up she climbed along the cave walls until it began to curve and then she was a lizard. She crawled across the cave ceiling, then descended down a stalactite, leaping at the last second. Again, in mid-air, she transformed into a cat and landed on all fours back in the circle. The crowd cheered. As she spun around, she transformed into a horse and kicked behind her. Then she rolled and shifted into a dragon and blew fire above the crowd.

Adrian's heart jumped in his throat. Anna had exposed herself in front of a crowd. She had promised him she'd be careful. That she wouldn't tell a soul what she was. What he was. She had betrayed his confidence. Betrayed herself.

Adrian glanced at Lola. She was examining him as he watched the footage. Dissecting his every movement. Did she know what he was too?

"Anna's our best fighter," she said.

Adrian turned back to the screen. Finally, Anna shifted back into sheep form, curling up into a tiny ball, as if none of it had happened. The crowd stood and cheered. She bowed.

"She's taught many new pledges skills that have kept them out of the alien's clutches."

The room spun. Adrian's stomach lurched and he nearly fell over. He wheezed in a breath. Anna, his girlfriend, the person he cared more about than anyone in the entire world, wasn't just a rebel supporter, but a leader. A fighter.

"How long?" he asked.

"We told her it was dangerous reconnecting with you, but she insisted." Lola turned off the screen and put a hand on Adrian's shoulder. A hand that suddenly had fingers made of keys. "Us shapeshifters need to stick together," she said. "Before it's really too late."

The color drained from Adrian's face. She was a shifter too. She knew Anna was a shifter and now he knew for certain that she knew he was one too. *God damn it, Anna.*

His heart pounded as Lola continued to stare at him. He wouldn't admit it. And yet he knew she knew the truth.

"It's already too late. They have Anna. I don't understand how she could do this to herself—to me."

"But don't you see? She didn't do it to you or to herself. She did it for everyone stuck in that prison. For all of us underground. For the future of our planet and people."

"You sound like Jack."

Lola shut her eyes and took a breath. "I know you want to help her. Anna's a part of our family too. We don't want anything to happen to her either. But this is the reality of our world. None of us get to run away. We don't get to pretend it isn't happening." Lola's eyes flicked to his watch, the way they had the first time she met him. "Your parents understood that."

Adrian instinctually grabbed his wrist with the watch on it, his insides churning. "You knew my parents?"

She nodded and walked over to the middle portion of blueprints. Upon closer inspection, he could see they were the uncompleted layout of the alien's lair.

"Your parents got the closest of any of us to figuring out how to disable the alien's energy source. With your mother's scientific knowledge and your father's technical prowess, they were unstoppable. Or so we thought."

"My father made watches. My mom studied plants. Sure, they believed in the cause, but—"

"But ordinary people can't do extraordinary things?" Lola turned to look at him now, her eyes half-lidded, curious and intense at the same time.

Adrian opened and shut his mouth. That wasn't what he was saying. But surely he knew his parents better than she thought she did. Didn't he?

"If you want to help Anna, you need to help all of us. Warden is a privileged position. You're in a lot of meetings. Make a lot of decisions on what happens to the prisoners. You also have the closest access to the aliens. We've been collecting weapons and getting more followers to our cause every week. But it all means nothing if we don't know what the aliens are planning. If we can't truly find their weakness. That's where you come in."

"And what about Anna?"

"You feed us information and we'll have a much better idea of how to get her out. But we can't make any rash decisions. We play it cool until we have enough intel to strike."

"And you're sure we can get her out?"

"With your help, yes."

Adrian thought of what Blood Cry said earlier about betting he would have already been captured for trying to rescue Anna. He knew it was true that he couldn't do it alone. That this group had information and skills that could help him get her back.

"Okay, then I'm in. But only to rescue Anna. I'm not joining your rebellion."

Lola gave him a curt nod. "Understood."

Adrian found himself taking a deep breath in, his shoulders relaxing for the first time all day. "So what do you need me to do?"

"Tomorrow all you need to do is go to work as usual. Every day after work you'll come here to train. We'll feed the plan to you little by little. And you'll report back."

"Train? Why do I need training?"

"Better to be prepared for any situation than to find yourself in a situation unprepared, right?"

Adrian nodded and got up. "Sure. I guess so."

"Oh and one other thing. It's important you don't involve anyone else in this mission. No matter how much you trust them. Not even friends."

THE NEXT DAY at work, Adrian kept his head down as he clocked in. He wasn't sure what would come out of his mouth if he had to talk to someone.

Zeke fell into stride with him. "What happened last night, man?"

Adrian tensed. "Last night? Nothing. Why?"

Zeke raised an eyebrow. "I waited outside your apartment for an hour before you texted me. Where were you?"

Adrian's stomach dropped. "I'm sorry. Would have texted you sooner, but the service was awful."

"Where?"

Adrian realized he was talking himself into a hole. "Uh, I got food poisoning." He hoped that would be the end of the conversation.

"But we ate the same thing for lunch and you were supposed to wait for me to eat dinner."

"I had a snack—lasagna."

"Lasagna." Zeke grabbed Adrian's shoulder and forced him to a standstill. "What's going on, man? What about the plan?"

"I meant to tell you. Anna called last night. Her cousin had a baby and she went to help her. She's fine."

Zeke let out a sound somewhere between a scoff and a laugh. "I don't know what's going on with you, but friends don't stand up friends. Not cool, man. I've gotta get back to work." With that, he turned and walked toward the entrance.

Adrian's shoulders sank in a strange mixture of relief and shame. He had never lied to his friend before. He had never really lied to anyone. He had kept one secret—being a shapeshifter—but never a flat-out lie. He realized he had better get good at it fast if he was going to keep up his end of the bargain and get Anna back.

Adrian settled into his office and examined his desk. The pile of papers from the day before had grown. It was the prisoner intake inbox. How had that many prisoners been sent in just one day?

The outbox beside it of prisoner releases was minuscule by comparison. There were barely any forms. Surely more prisoners would be up for parole by now.

Adrian took a few pages from the top of the intake pile. He skimmed the crime: all three were in for theft. And the conviction: twenty years.

Adrian furrowed his brow. That seemed harsh for mere theft. He turned the pages over; there was no other information on the crime.

He grabbed more pages from the pile and leafed through. A handful more of generic thefts and possession of illegal substances. All minor crimes, sentenced with fifteen, twenty, even fifty years in prison. Of all the crimes, there was only one murder. A dragon that ripped off an alien guard's mask. This was the only crime for which there were vivid details. And the conviction: a life sentence.

Well, that was the only intake that seemed to make any sense. He set that one at the bottom of the pile and started back at the top. From the drawer, he retrieved a pile of appeal forms and got to work.

A few forms in, the familiar clanking of Caesar's metallic parts carried through the door. Adrian got up and opened the door before he knocked. "Good morning, Caesar."

"Greetings, Warden Walker. May I be of service?"

"Actually, yeah. Come in, come in." Adrian stepped back and let Caesar pass. He stood front and center on the other side of the desk.

Adrian sat back down and held up a few of the intake papers. "Where did all these new prisoners come from? The pile was half as large last night."

"They are criminals who have been brought to justice."

"I know, but I mean how did this many people get arrested in one night? Was there another rally?"

"It is not in my programming to tell you."

"But you know, then?"

"I am a robot, warden. I do not know anything. I am given orders and follow them. Will that be all?"

Adrian realized there was no point in pressing him. "That's all. Thanks, Caesar."

After work, Adrian took the subway home, stood before the door, and then turned around. Anna wasn't there to hear his knock. She wasn't there to have dinner with him or watch TV or talk about their days. So what was the point of going home?

Adrian found himself in the alley with the door leading to the rebels. He shifted into rabbit form and knocked. Blood Cry was there to greet him again. "Ready for your first day of training?"

Adrian shrugged.

Blood Cry jabbed his shoulder playfully. "Your enthusiasm is contagious."

"Is Lola here? I have information for her."

"She won't be back until tomorrow. Best you keep it to yourself until then."

"Where is she?"

"I'm going to keep that to myself for now."

"You don't trust me, do you?"

"It's not about trust. It's about strategy. Everyone has a little bit of information. Very few people have a lot of it. It's how we stay safe until the day comes."

"What day comes?"

"You'll see."

Blood Cry led him into an open room with a mat covering the floor. He shut the door behind him.

"You wanna talk about trust? Show me what you've got."

"What do you mean?"

"Make this a fair fight. Make yourself a dragon."

Adrian gaped at Blood Cry. Was he flat out asking him to shapeshift?

Blood Cry cracked his neck left and right. "You can keep hiding it or you can use it to your advantage. Either way, I'm coming at you in three, two . . ."

He started toward Adrian.

On instinct, Adrian cowered on the spot, arms protecting his head.

Still in motion, Blood Cry's tail swiped Adrian's shoulder. He slowed just in time to not hit the wall.

"All right, that's one way to play it. Stand up now."

Adrian uncovered his head and hesitated.

"Don't worry, let's start simple. Stand up and put your hands up."

Adrian did as Blood Cry instructed.

"I'm coming at you slowly this time. In three, two . . ." Blood Cry charged at him before one.

Adrian took off for the opposite corner of the room.

"Oh come on now." Blood Cry halted and threw up his arms.

Adrian skirted along the wall toward the door. "I just don't see how this is going to help me get Anna back."

And with that, he left.

Center for Dangerous Hybrid Control
Prisoner Intake Form
CDHC
Name: Gregory Grizzly
Date: 9-16-3050
Crime: Theft
Conviction: 20 years
Statement:

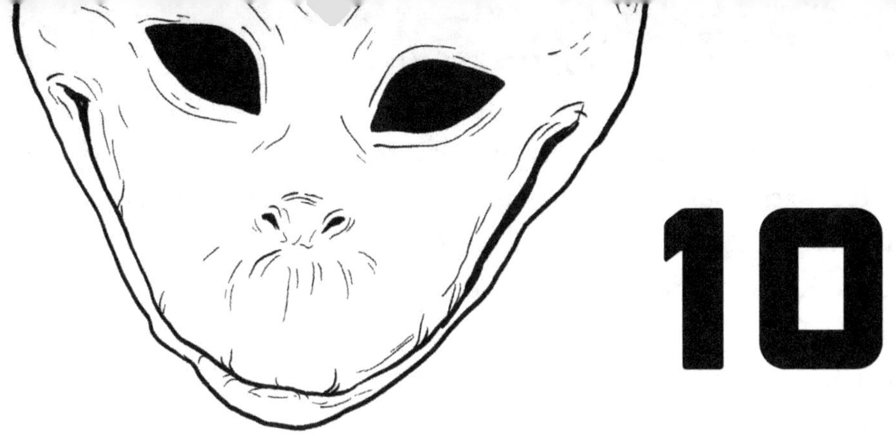

10

THE PILE ON Adrian's desk was now a mountain of papers. This had to mean hundreds more prisoners had been captured in the past week alone. Adrian ruffled through the top papers—again, no details as to the crimes. Again, grossly disproportionate sentences.

Adrian was warden. He was put in charge. And if Caesar wasn't going to clue him in, he'd go straight to the person who hired him. He grabbed a stack of papers and left his office.

Adrian walked through the overgrown path to the alien compound. He knocked on the steel door and waited.

"State your purpose," a cool voice said seemingly from all around him.

"Uh, this is the warden. I would like to speak to Jack."

"Do you have a meeting scheduled?"

"Well, no, but—"

"Hold please."

Adrian paced before the door for what seemed like an hour. Suddenly, the door to the decontamination chamber opened.

The voice settled around him again, "You may enter."

Adrian walked in and endured the annoying process, finally putting on an oxygen suit and stepping into the central room. He followed the hallway Caesar had led him down last time, and after a couple of wrong turns, found himself in front of Jack's office.

His heartbeat sped as he thought of Anna on the other side of the door. He wasn't sure he'd be able to ignore her again. The door slid open before he could collect himself.

"Greetings, Warden Walker. You may enter."

Jack sat upright at her desk, her eyes boring into Adrian's. He dared not look anywhere else as he smiled and walked in. The door shut behind him.

"Thank you for seeing me," Adrian started, chancing a look around the room—the empty room. Anna was not there. His heart clenched. Anything could have happened to her.

"Anything for the man overseeing the prison. So?" She looked as expectant as someone without eyebrows could look.

"Right. Well." Adrian fanned the intake forms across her desk. "It's the strangest thing. There's been a drastic increase in prisoners this week, and even stranger, their crimes are all similar. Whoever is filling out the forms is not doing a thorough job."

Jack stared at the papers for but an instant. "Thank you for bringing this to my attention, warden. There has indeed been an increase in prisoners. We accepted transfers from a neighboring city. My guards must have gotten lazy filling out that many forms."

"I should have been informed," Adrian said. "Our facilities were already nearing max capacity. Now they're definitely overcrowded. We can't sustain this."

"You're absolutely right, warden. I think we can find a good solution for everyone here."

Adrian picked up one of the forms—a man who got fifty years for stealing a piece of bread. "Look at this. And there are more like it. We could go back through the crimes—reduce sentences for at least half of the inmates. Maye even pardon some of them today."

"Pardon?" Jack sat even straighter in her chair. Adrian had to look up to make eye contact now. "A crime is a crime. We cannot release criminals back into society willy-nilly. They must serve their time."

"I know, but my point is the punishment doesn't fit the crime—"

"I have another solution." Jack stood. "By the end of the month, a third of the prisoners will be transferred to our newest location."

"Where's that?"

"Nearby."

"Should I come to see it? I can sort the prisoners, recommend who would be a good fit to move—"

"Not to worry. I will handle the details. You only need to worry about your job."

Adrian's mouth gaped. Wasn't *this* his job?

Jack walked to the door as it slid open. "Thank you for coming by."

Adrian gathered the papers on her desk and walked across the threshold. Caesar was waiting on the other side. "Greetings, warden," he said.

"Oh and next time, warden, make sure Caesar escorts you to my office," Jack said before the door shut.

Adrian reluctantly followed Caesar back to his office. He had been so concerned about talking to Jack, about seeing Anna again, that he hadn't thought to look around. What if she had been in one of those rooms? What if . . . ?

His mind wandered to the shapeshifter he had seen banging on the door in agony. There was something Jack wasn't telling him. Something that could mean the end of Anna. And he was going to find out.

■ ■ ■

Adrian could hardly contain himself when Blood Cry met him at the underground entrance. The door had barely shut behind him before he said, "I need to see Lola immediately. Something really weird is going on at the prison."

"That's gonna be a bit difficult tonight."

"Don't tell me she's out again?"

Blood Cry gestured for Adrian to follow. When they reached the tunnel's outlet, Adrian's jaw dropped. A sea of hybrids had moved into the town below. Hundreds more than the last time Adrian had visited. Where had they all come from?

Once they reached the base of the cave, they joined the crowd. Adrian stayed close to Blood Cry as people made way for him to walk past. There were so many of them—dogs, cats, bears, horses—any hybrid you could ever come across was present.

"The aliens have been cracking down. Finding any excuse in the book to lock innocent people up. They've been coming down here by the dozens."

Adrian's stomach twisted. His fears were confirmed. He gripped his bag, which held a handful of the bogus intake forms he tried to show Jack.

Lola appeared on a raised platform several feet in front of them. Blood Cry kept leading him closer as she began to talk over the anxious voices. "If I could have your attention." Her shout was absorbed into the din.

Blood Cry signaled to a gorilla standing behind Lola and he let out a rumbling roar that settled the room into silence.

Lola gave an encouraging smile. "I know you're all scared," she said. "But you're safe now. We've built this sanctuary so we have a chance. To keep living. To fight back."

She looked out over the crowd, seeming to make eye contact with each hybrid. "In order to do so, we all need to work together." Her eyes seemed to settle on Adrian as she said this. "We must share resources. Help with tasks of daily living. Lend our skills to our neighbors.

"For those of you who have been down here longest, remember how it felt to arrive. Be hospitable until we can build accommodations for our new friends. We are all in this together."

"What about our families?" someone shouted. "They're locking us up for no reason!"

The crowd echoed the sentiment.

Lola put her hand up to silence the crowd, but the noise only seemed to increase. Even the gorilla's roar did nothing to quell their shouts.

Lola's mouth still moved, but her words were lost to the crowd. She opened and shut her mouth. For the first time since Adrian had met her, she seemed to have lost control. Her eyes searched the restless crowd as if she was looking for a solution.

Adrian pushed past the few bodies separating him from the stage and hoisted himself up. "I have proof," he shouted, though he knew no one could hear him. He fumbled with his bag and pulled out a few of the intake forms. "Proof!" he shouted again.

The first few rows quieted down. Like a row of dominos, slowly the crowd settled into silence from front to back.

"You're right," Adrian said, his voice cracking from trying to project. He looked down at the first form and read, "Jerry Bookkeeper, convicted of breaking and entering. Sentence: life in prison."

"That's my husband," someone wailed from the crowd.

Adrian's hands shook as he switched to the next paper. "Harold Patricks, convicted of theft. Sentence: fifty years."

"That's our dad!" a few voices shouted from the center of the crowd.

Adrian turned to the next paper. "Katarina Drillius, convicted of disrespecting a guard. Sentence: sixty years."

"That's my girlfriend," a man in the front row raised his fist in the air. Adrian met his eyes and felt his heart clench as he thought of Anna.

"They are locking people up for no reason but yelling at Lola or fighting each other isn't going to do any good."

Lola placed a hand on Adrian's shoulder. "Thank you, Adrian."

He stepped back and let her continue.

"The aliens may be able to lock us up, but this is still our home turf. We will fight back. We will. But not tonight. We are only as strong as our weakest link. So let's make sure all of us get enough food and rest to be healthy."

The crowd dispersed quietly. All but for two bears Adrian recognized. Corky and Coco were waiting at the edge of the stage, tears welling in their eyes.

"Mr. Adrian, we were hoping you could give this letter to our father," Corky said.

"Oh, I . . ."

Coco added, "We don't know if we'll ever see him again. His name is Gregory."

"He looks like us." Corky pushed the letter into Adrian's hand. "Please."

"Okay, I'll try," Adrian said, not sure what else to say.

The twins' eyes lit up. They hugged each other and scampered off toward their mother, who was waiting at the edge of the crowd.

Lola placed a hand on Adrian's shoulder and guided him off the stage and into her office. She shut the door and turned to him, smiling. "Thank you for what you did."

"I tried to tell you yesterday."

"Now you know why I was unavailable."

"I don't know how you do it," Adrian shook his head. "All those people. How do you even know where to go?"

"We have our ways. I'm hoping you'll be one of them."

"I tried confronting Jack about the influx of prisoners, but she dodged my questions. They're moving them soon. I don't know where. And Anna—I don't know where she is now."

"Anna is resilient. She's trained. She'll hold out. Unfortunately, many of the other prisoners won't."

Adrian threw up his arms. "Well, what can I do? Jack basically told me not to do my job. I'm just supposed to sit at my desk and pretend, I guess. I won't be able to get away with anything."

Lola smiled again. "This is what I was waiting for. I was waiting for you to be ready to help us. So here's what you're going to do tomorrow."

11

UNLOCK A CELL. That's all he had to do. Unlock one cell so a rebel could sneak six prisoners into the underground. It was simple enough.

But Adrian couldn't stop thinking about Warden Philly. The unlocked cell that sent Adrian to the supply closet. The knowledge that Warden Philly was working for the rebel cause. Would history repeat itself?

Adrian's hand shook as he brought his morning coffee to his lips. He waited silently in his office for Caesar to do his morning rounds. Both the intake and outtake bins were empty today. Surely Jack had ordered it. Adrian had confronted her and his punishment was a time out. No work for the warden today. Only work for the rebel. Temporary rebel, that is.

Adrian's leg bounced involuntarily. Ten o'clock. 10:05. 10:10. Usually Caesar's motor hummed at the door by now.

After another five minutes, Adrian got up and opened the door himself.

"Greetings, warden!"

"Ah!" Adrian stumbled backward as Caesar wheeled inside, the familiar hum absent. "You're so quiet," he said.

"Indeed," Caesar said. "I have been retrofitted with the Whisper 9000. The robotics team has been salvaging and refurbishing much technology."

Adrian had never heard of the Whisper 9000, but he did remember commercials for a quiet vacuum cleaner before the aliens came. He wondered what Caesar meant by "salvaging."

"That's great, Caesar," he said. "Do you have any orders for me today?"

"None, warden. Please resume your usual duties." With that, Caesar left.

His usual duties? Adrian didn't even know what those were anymore.

Caesar wouldn't be checking on him again until the late afternoon. This was his window.

Adrian slipped out of his office and began to walk the grounds. No one would question the warden making rounds.

He wandered for a while, passing enclosure after enclosure that were now packed full of hybrids. Most of the cells were too out in the open. He needed to find one no one would notice. One that could be unlocked for a few hours until closing.

Then he remembered Coco and Corky's letter—the letter he was supposed to give to their father. If he unlocked his cell, they could be reunited. Gregory, they had said. A bear.

Adrian thought back to when he was a janitor making his rounds. There were several bears he remembered, but one specifically the same auburn color as Corky and Coco. His cell was toward the entrance of the prison, which meant higher visibility but a faster exit. He would have to wait until closer to closing.

Adrian went back to his office and shut the door. It would be a boring day, a nerve-wracking day, but he had a plan now. One he could implement easily and quickly.

Adrian waited for hours. He replayed the plan over and over in his head: wait five minutes longer than usual, walk slowly so others clocked out before him and the guards would be in the middle of changing shifts, and then make a quick detour to unlock the cell.

Finally, the clock struck five after five. Adrian straightened the sparse items on his desk. He adjusted his shirt and put on his coat, patting the pocket that held the letter. Then he started his walk toward the cell.

He focused on syncing his breath with his step. Left, inhale. Right, exhale. Left, inhale. Right, exhale. No need to be nervous. Left, inhale. Right, exhale. He had the master key to all the locks. Left, inhale. Right, exhale. It wouldn't take him more than thirty seconds. Left, inhale, Right, exhale.

Adrian sped up as a guard passed him. He had to catch the lull between the shift change.

The exit was in sight. So was the cell. And Gregory, who was hunched in the corner reading. Adrian slowly gravitated toward the cell, his eyes fixed on Gregory. How could he get his attention?

He cleared his throat, but none of the prisoners looked up. Then he coughed. First one cough, then a few in a row. Finally, one of the prisoners noticed him and straightened up, nudging his friend. Gregory was the last to look up.

Adrian widened his eyes at him and brought a finger to his lips to indicate they should be quiet.

Gregory dropped his book and shot up, tugging on the other prisoners to quiet down.

Adrian met Gregory at the bars.

"Hi," Gregory whispered, surprise in his voice.

"Hi," Adrian whispered back, revealing the key in his hand and the letter.

Gregory's eyes widened.

"They're coming for you," Adrian said as he inserted the key into the lock. "Don't get noticed tonight."

Gregory nodded and took the letter. The other prisoners exchanged looks. For the first time since Adrian had taken his job so many years ago as a janitor, he saw hope in their eyes.

Suddenly, a hand was on Adrian's shoulder. "What's going on over here?"

Adrian froze under Zeke's grip, the key halfway turned in the lock. He spun to meet his friend. "Just checking the locks is all."

"Checking the locks? That's not your job anymore."

"Old habits die hard." Adrian gave a half chuckle.

Zeke raised an eyebrow. "I know what's going on here."

Adrian held his breath. Between standing him up for dinner and this, he was sure Zeke had him figured out.

"You need a guys night out!"

Adrian let out his breath. "I do?"

"Yeah, you've been taking this warden stuff way too seriously. Bailing on our dinner. Worrying about Anna. Now these locks? Leave it to the guards and come with me." Zeke took the keys from him and re-locked the cell.

Before Adrian knew what was happening, Zeke was leading him toward the exit. Adrian glanced back at the prisoners and Gregory to see that hope had once again been replaced by apprehension.

He had failed.

■ ■ ■

It was nine p.m. by the time Adrian reached the underground. "I'm sorry," he said in a heaving breath. Blood Cry let him in without a word.

Adrian followed him down the now-familiar tunnel. "I almost got caught. I got down here as soon as I could."

Blood Cry remained silent as he led Adrian to Lola's office.

She sat, not unlike Jack, behind her desk. The warm smile he had grown accustomed to each time she greeted him was absent.

A pit grew in Adrian's stomach as he sat down across from her. He waited for her to speak first, but the silence got to him. "I almost unlocked the cell, but a guard—my friend, Zeke—he caught on. I had to go with him or it would have looked suspicious. I got down here as soon as I could. Is everyone okay?"

"Yash was captured," Lola said.

The pit in Adrian's stomach rose. He inhaled sharply to keep from throwing up. "I'm sorry, I'm sorry," he said. "I'll find out where Yash is tomorrow. We can rescue him and try again."

Lola rested her hand on the desk. "We need to take a beat, Adrian. Every action we take for the cause has a consequence, a risk. All of us know it. Yash knew. Anna knew. And now you do too."

Adrian nodded, unsure of what to say next.

Lola continued. "Tomorrow, you'll go to work like normal. Do nothing out of the ordinary. Do you understand?"

Adrian nodded again.

"The best thing you can do is to continue your training with Blood Cry. Continue to prepare. You're still our inside man, but it does no good if you're found out too."

Lola stood and Adrian mimicked her. "I'll see you tomorrow."

Blood Cry was waiting for him outside of Lola's office. "You ready?"

■ ■ ■

Adrian found himself back in the training room, Blood Cry across from him.

"This'll work better if we're an even match," Blood Cry said. "If you're not ready to, then—"

"No, I'm ready." Adrian held his breath and imagined a dragon of similar stature to Blood Cry. His limbs cramped as they extended and bulged, his skin itched as scales overtook the current fur. Just as Blood Cry made contact with his torso, his stomach twisted, assuring him the transformation was complete. He stumbled backward but didn't fall.

Blood Cry whistled. "Well done. It's almost like looking in a mirror."

Heat rose to Adrian's cheeks. He was glad the scales could hide the color. He had shapeshifted in front of a stranger. In front of someone who already knew what he was, but still. He felt naked. He felt more vulnerable than when he was a sheep or a cat or even a rabbit. Because what no one but Anna knew was that dragon was his original form.

"The key is to embrace your shape," Blood Cry went on. "Your greatest assets as a dragon are what?"

Adrian looked down at his clawed fingers, opened his mouth, and felt the fire building within. "Fire," he said, accidentally spitting out an ember.

"That's one. What else?"

Adrian held up his claws.

"Sure, but dogs have claws; so do bears and eagles."

Adrian looked down at his toes and scanned his scaley body. "I'm big," he finally said.

Blood Cry chuckled and spun around. "Notice anything?" His thick tail swung from one side of the room to the other.

"Tail," Adrian said. "Of course."

"Give it a swing."

Adrian glanced back to make sure it was there—it was. He focused on it and felt it wiggle.

Blood Cry emitted a knowing hum. "And there you have it. Shapeshifters are all smoke and mirrors. You can look like anything, transform into anything. But you don't know your own body." He nudged Adrian's tail with his foot. Adrian reflexively pulled it away.

"There you go!" Blood Cry took a step back. "Your main obstacle is to learn how to use your various shapes. To master them. Until then, you're useless."

Adrian clenched his fists. He shifted his tail to the left and then swiveled with all his might toward Blood Cry.

In one swift motion, Blood Cry caught his tail and twisted it so Adrian found himself face down on the floor with a thud that knocked the wind out of him.

Blood Cry chuckled and held out his claw to Adrian.

Once he'd caught his breath, Adrian accepted his help up.

"Now you know how your greatest asset can be used against you. Try again."

Adrian wiggled his hips, getting used to the heavy tail behind him.

"Atta boy," Blood Cry said. "Give me your best shot."

Adrian shook away the ache from his blind tail swing. This time, he wound up like he was going to do the same, and then at the last second, he swung the other way.

Blood Cry didn't see it coming. He landed on the ground with an "Oompf!"

Adrian steadied himself. The blow had taken almost as much out of him as it did from Blood Cry.

He waited for the dragon to get back on his feet. "Not bad," Blood Cry said. "A little clumsy, but it did the trick."

Adrian couldn't help but feel proud of himself.

Blood Cry returned to his fighting stance. "Now let's refine it."

For the next hour, Adrian mirrored Blood Cry's movements. Every swing of the tail, every breath of fire, every swipe of his claws. With each move, Adrian felt more and more at ease in his dragon's skin.

Each night he returned and worked with Blood Cry. And each night Blood Cry brought along a different hybrid. He learned how to maximize his agility as a rabbit, his strength as a bear, his speed as a horse. Everyone had their own strategies and Adrian learned them all. He no longer felt fear or embarrassment at his shapeshifting. In fact, even the discomfort ebbed as he regularly transformed.

Adrian felt more invigorated at work too. Even though Jack had stripped him of all responsibilities, he had something to look forward to. And he was getting stronger, so when the day came, he'd be able to rescue Anna. For now, following orders and helping the rebels was his best bet.

A **DRIAN FELT BETTER** than he'd ever felt in his body. Even as a sheep he could feel the leanness in his muscles, the stability in his legs that had developed since his training started. He waved to Zeke as he entered the prison for another monotonous day at the office. It was all adding up to something, he had to remember that.

He meandered toward Gregory's cell, as he did every other morning to smile and let him and the others know help was still on the way. But the cell was empty.

Adrian's smile withered. A pit formed in his stomach. He looked around at the neighboring cells—at least three of them were empty.

Where had they all gone? They weren't supposed to be transferred to the new location for another week.

Adrian rushed back to Zeke at the entrance.

"Where are the prisoners?" he asked.

Zeke's brow furrowed. "What do you mean?"

"The prisoners in these front cells. They're gone."

"Oh yeah. I think they were transferred."

"Transferred where? I didn't get any memos."

"I don't know, man."

Adrian realized it was pointless to ask him any more questions. He rushed to his office and waited at the door for Caesar to check in.

An hour went by, and finally he appeared. "Greetings, warden. May I be of—"

"I'd like to see Jack." Adrian could barely contain himself.

"Fearless Leader is very busy currently," Caesar said.

"It's important. I need to see her today."

"Very well." Caesar turned and sailed out the door.

Adrian hesitated, wondering if he should wait for him to return, but decided to follow.

Soon enough, he was back inside the alien lair.

Jack sat behind her desk, as usual. Again, no Anna beside her.

"Adrian, what can I do for you?"

"I, uh, I noticed some prisoners were missing from their cells."

"Oh, don't worry about that. They were transferred early. Isn't that what you wanted, more space in the prison?"

"But where have they been transferred?"

"To another facility."

"Yes, but where?"

Jack smiled.

"As warden, I'd like to visit it," Adrian said, his voice nearly wavering as he stared into Jack's stony eyes.

Suddenly the door swished open. Anna walked right past him and whispered into Jack's ear. She nodded and said, "Excuse me for a moment." She stood and walked out the door, leaving him and Anna alone.

Adrian's heart raced. He couldn't believe it. He lunged to hug her but her hands caught his shoulder.

"We don't have much time," she hissed. "The aliens are growing stronger."

"Did they hurt you? Are you okay?"

Anna glanced over his shoulder. "The new location is here."

"What do you mean?"

She looked down at the floor. "Here."

"Show me."

She shook her head. "They've made a breakthrough with their experiments. They've figured out how to breathe."

"What do you mean? They can already breathe."

"In *our* atmosphere. Tell Lola she needs to act fast. Before they can distribute it. Tell her they've moved on from shapeshifters. They're going to exterminate everyone."

"I'm going to get you out of here," Adrian said.

Anna dropped her shoulders and resumed her position next to Jack's desk. He sat down just as Jack reentered.

"Well, it seems this meeting needs to be over. If you'd like to see the new location, I can show you, warden." There was a threatening edge in her voice. Her eyes dissected him as she waited for his reply.

Adrian dared not glance at Anna. "I should get back to work. I trust you've made the right decision in transferring the prisoners. Thank you for listening when I told you about the overcrowding."

"Certainly. And if you need anything else, my door is always open."

It took everything in him not to glance back at Anna as he left with Caesar. All he knew was that continuing to pry would only bring more danger. If he wanted to get Anna out, he had to deliver her message to Lola.

■ ■ ■

Adrian got to the underground early. He knew Blood Cry wouldn't be waiting at the door but tried knocking anyway. As he waited, he examined the one-sided lock. There was no way to open it from this side—a smart safety move on the part of the rebels. But the sooner Adrian could get inside tonight, the better.

He glanced around the alley. As far as he could tell it was empty. He focused on his left hand and imagined it was thin enough to fit through the gap between the door and the threshold. Almost instantly, his hand cramped more intensely than ever before. His fingers flattened, then his palm. Adrian leaned against the door to hide his hand as he slid it through the gap and felt for the keyhole. His breath grew heavy as he imagined his index finger molding to the keyhole's shape. He had never double-shifted before. In fact, he didn't even know if it was possible. Pain shot through his finger and instinct caused him to retract it from the keyhole. He gritted his teeth and tried again. This time, he breathed through the pain. When he heard the click of the lock, he knew it had worked.

As the door cracked open, he released his finger and hand from their uncomfortable position, shaking them back into their usual form.

Adrian managed to cross the threshold and shut the door, leaning against it as he caught his breath.

He had double-shifted. It *was* possible. He wondered if Lola knew. And remembered there was so much she didn't know.

He mustered his strength and ran through the tunnels toward her office.

He burst in without knocking. But it was empty.

Adrian wandered the halls and headed back toward the mess hall. Anyone he came across he asked, "Have you seen Lola?"

All of them shook their heads, "No."

It was Blood Cry he found first, helping himself to an early dinner.

Adrian didn't bother to say hello. "Where's Lola?" he asked.

Blood Cry paused mid-bite on a potato. "You're early."

"Where's Lola?" Adrian asked again.

"This is becoming a pattern, you know. Barging in here looking for our leader. There are channels."

"Screw the channels! This time tomorrow, the aliens will have wiped out everyone at the prison—probably me included."

A clatter sounded at a neighboring table. Adrian looked to the noise and saw a rabbit, paw suspended in the air above a dropped fork. There were three others at her table. And at least ten others in the room—including Gregory's children, Corky and Coco. They had all heard.

Adrian's stomach dropped as he watched their faces pale.

Blood Cry stood and clutched Adrian's shoulder. "When I say there are channels, I mean there are channels." He straightened and smiled wider than Adrian had ever seen. "Not to worry, folks. We're going to clear all of this up. Get back to your meals."

Blood Cry gestured toward the exit. Adrian started to follow, but suddenly Lola appeared, brow furrowed.

"I was just coming to find you," Blood Cry said.

"You forgot this is a cave. Everything echoes."

Adrian's face grew hot. His outcry had sent the entire mess hall into either tears or urgent whispers.

"Blood Cry, send word for everyone to gather in the mess hall." Lola gestured for Adrian to sit. "They've already heard the worst of it. So let's figure out what we're going to do about it now. All of us, together."

As more people gathered, Adrian told her everything that had happened and everything he knew. His meetings with Jack, the ever-moving energy source, what Anna had told him, the number of prisoners still there, the number of guards. He drew a map of the location of the alien lair, filling in as many gaps as he could. He guessed where the experimentation area would be. He told them about Caesar.

"I know he's programmed with a map of the entire lair. Any time he's taken me there, it's like he's following GPS directions."

"Do you think he could lead you to the energy source?" Lola asked.

Adrian shook his head. "There's no way he'd do what I ask. Jack is the only one who can control him and he isn't programmed to have free will. Every morning and evening he comes to check on me. And if he catches on at all to what we're doing, we'll be goners."

"What's his model?" Someone called from a few tables over. Adrian stood to see the owner of the voice. The woman stood too. She was a cat, one that looked strangely familiar to him even though he was certain they'd never met.

"Have you seen a number engraved on the back of his head?" she asked.

"A number?"

"I worked for Robotics Inc. before the aliens came. They took all our models and modified them. If you know the model, I can try to figure out what operating system he has."

Something clicked in Adrian's head. "The Whisper 9000," he said.

"That's not a model number," the woman said.

"No, I know. Caesar told me they retrofitted him with the Whisper 9000."

"Like the vacuum cleaner?" Lola asked.

Adrian nodded.

A man stood further down the table. "Well, I don't know how to download the map, but if he's running on a Whisper 9000, I could show you how to disable him."

"Not so fast," the cat said. "I never said I needed to know his operating system to tell him how to get the map." She pulled out a piece of paper and started drawing a diagram. "But in the meantime, might as well give him a backup plan."

For the first time in a long time, Adrian felt lighter. They could do this. They could get people out, including Anna.

"We also need to figure out how to break out the prisoners," Lola said. "I'm assuming you only have one master set of keys."

Adrian nodded.

"Shapeshifters, you know who you are. I know it's a lot to ask you to leave the safety of the underground, so I won't ask all of you. Anyone willing to help, please raise your hands."

Adrian looked around. Everyone else in the room was looking around at one another, expressions anxious, curious, or nervous. Slowly, one hand went into the air. Then another. Ten people in total eventually had their hands in the air, including the rabbit who had dropped her fork.

"All of you, gather by the far table. Adrian will show you how to shift your fingers into the master key."

Adrian's stomach flipped. He had never publicly announced himself as a shapeshifter and now all these people—hundreds of people—knew. He swallowed and headed toward the far table, meeting the other ten shifters there.

There was an assortment of mostly hybrid dogs, rabbits, and cats. Adrian realized most shapeshifters wouldn't dare spend much time as a more menacing hybrid like a bear or dragon—even if it was their original form.

Adrian set the master key on the table and held up his finger. He cleared his throat. "So, uh, you just . . ." He shut his eyes and imagined the master key. When the familiar cramping subsided, he opened his eyes.

Some of them were looking wide-eyed at him, while others whispered nervously.

"You picture it in your mind's eye and then it should appear."

"Like this?" A tall cat in the back of the group raised her hand, where the key now replaced her finger.

"Exactly!"

A few more of them got it immediately, holding up their key fingers proudly.

"It's not working," a boy in monkey form said.

Adrian grabbed the key and walked over to him. "Try holding it." He handed the boy the key. "Now hold up your other hand and close your eyes."

The boy did as he said.

"Now feel the shape of the key, picture its shape in your head. Got that?"

The boy nodded.

"Now imagine your finger transforming into the shape of the key."

The boy winced as his finger pulsed.

"That's it! Keep imagining it. Breathe through the pain."

The boy inhaled sharply and his finger continued to pulse. After a few minutes, the pulsing began to shift into the shape of the key. The boy gave a gasp and opened his eyes.

"I did it," he said.

"You did it." Adrian patted him on the back.

Everyone else who hadn't transformed yet seemed to visibly relax. By the end of the hour, every single one of them had successfully transformed their fingers into the key. What's more, there were now double the number of people at the table.

Lola appeared beside Adrian. "Well done, everyone. It's getting late and we have a big day ahead. We'll gather at first light and commence our plan." She turned to Adrian. "I want you to go home, get some rest. Go to work as usual tomorrow. We'll signal you when it's time."

She wrapped her arms around him in a light hug. "We're glad to have you on our side."

Adrian's stomach fluttered. "We'll get Anna out too, right?"

Lola straightened. "You said you know where they're keeping her. We'll do everything in our power to get her out."

Adrian's stomach settled until Corky and Coco appeared in front of him. "Um, Mr. Adrian," one said. "Did you give our father the letter?"

"I did," he said, his voice laced with regret. "I'm going to find him."

"We want to help," the other one said. "Lola says we're too young to come."

"We want to be brave like you!" said the first.

Brave like him. Adrian suddenly felt like an imposter. He bent down so he was at their eye level, fighting the nagging feeling in his neck. "Sometimes being brave means knowing your strengths and weaknesses. It means letting other people do the things you wish you could do because when you're doing what you do best, that helps everyone, right?"

The twins nodded as if trying to convince themselves.

"Which of you wrote that letter?" Adrian asked.

"We wrote it together," they said in unison.

"There you go. The two of you can be the official historical recordkeepers. You can tell the story of what happens here. And how we beat the aliens. How does that sound?"

The twins' eyes widened. "Yeah!"

"Go gather your supplies, then."

The twins hurried off. A few others said goodbye to him and then he walked with Blood Cry to the exit.

"Big day tomorrow," Blood Cry said. "Looks like our training will come in handy."

Adrian smiled but couldn't imagine actually shapeshifting in public. He left without another word, knowing he would not be able to sleep a wink.

Center for Dangerous Zoo
Bird Greenhouses
Auditorium
Display Cages
Prisoner Cells
Monkeys
Prisoner cells
Maintenance
Tickets
Entrance
Welcome Zoo
Admin
Warden's office

Hybrid Control
Map
Bears
Prisoner cells
Elephant and Giraffe Sanctuary
Alien Lair
Lions
Prisoner cells
Hippos
Prisoner cells

13

ADRIAN'S FEET FELT like rocks as he walked up to the prison entrance. His heart and breath were operating at three times their normal speed. He stopped and took a deep breath before walking across the threshold between his own freedom and Anna's.

He clocked in and waved to Zeke, who brightened and waved back. Adrian hesitated. Should he tell him what was going on? Warn him not to get involved? No, that would only endanger him more.

Adrian turned away and picked up his pace to his office. He left the door open and unfolded the paper in his pocket with the diagrams on how to download the map—and how to disable Caesar if worse came to worst.

Adrian bobbed his leg up and down, waiting for the robot to come to check on him. The dragons would wait for his signal to start a fire so Caesar wouldn't be able to alert the aliens.

It seemed like an eternity before Caesar came up to the door. "Greetings, warden!"

Adrian straightened and tried to act casual. "Good morning, Caesar."

"May I be of service?"

"Yes, come in, come in." Adrian shut the door behind Caesar and gestured to the chair across from his.

Before Caesar could sit, Adrian said, "Oh my gosh, Caesar, you're smoking!"

Caesar turned, trying to see his own backside. "I will run diagnostics."

"There's no time for that." Adrian yanked open the hatch on his back.

Caesar tried to turn again. "What are you doing?"

"Finding the problem," Adrian said as he extracted a drive from his pocket.

His motherboard looked different from any of the provided diagrams. Adrian tried hovering the drive over different areas, but none seemed to be the right connection. If he didn't do something—and fast—Caesar would run diagnostics and figure out he was lying.

He thought of what the ex-vacuum salesman had told him. Remove the fuse to the right of the motherboard. Adrian zeroed in on it and snapped it out of place.

Caesar teetered and fell face down with a clunk.

Adrian stood over him, panting. As he bent down, Caesar twitched and grabbed his arm. "I can't feel my legs!"

Adrenaline shot through Adrian. Removing the fuse was supposed to disable him.

"What did you do?" Caesar asked.

"Uh, I don't know." Which was true enough. Adrian left the dislodged fuse inside the hatch and closed it.

"I will alert the engineering team to retrieve me."

The engineering team? As far as Adrian knew, those were aliens. This meant instead of keeping the aliens away from the prisoners, they would be coming closer to all the action.

"No!" Adrian said it before he could stop himself. "I'll take you to them."

"Warden, you cannot carry 325 pounds of dead weight."

Adrian looked around wildly and remembered the package cart in his closet. "I'll take you on this."

"If you insist," Caesar said.

Adrian regretted not just putting Caesar's fuse back as he hoisted and pulled the robot onto the cart. But he couldn't risk Caesar finding out about their mission. He needed to get him as far away as possible and right now that meant the alien lair.

Adrian was sweating profusely by the time they reached the entrance to the lair. It was the hardest workout of his life. So hard he didn't bother looking back to see if the dragons had started the fire.

Caesar noticed it first. "My sensors detect smoke approximately one mile southwest."

"I'm sure—it's—nothing," Adrian huffed. "Can you—open—the door?"

"We should turn around and find the source. It could be a fire. Or a generator malfunction."

Adrian inhaled a big gulp of air and straightened. "I'll notify the janitor. Let's get you fixed."

Caesar did the robot equivalent of a shrug and opened the decontamination chamber.

The engineers were already waiting in the lobby when they reached the other side. "What happened?" one of them asked.

"He just collapsed," Adrian said.

"I thought I was smoking," Caesar added.

"Right. Yes, he was smoking."

The engineers furrowed their brows. Two of them took the cart from Adrian and wheeled it down the left hallway.

The third didn't follow. "Would you mind coming with us?" she asked. She was shorter than Jack by a head, her mouth not quite as wide, her eyes kinder.

"Oh, uh, I should get back to work."

"It would help to understand what happened so we can best fix Caesar." She held his gaze and he couldn't think of any more excuses besides getting back to work.

Adrian reluctantly followed them down the hall. There was a ding to his right, and two people stepped out of an elevator. "Going down," a female robot voice stated.

Adrian's heart leapt. Down. That was where Anna said the experiments were taking place. There was a chance that was where Jack kept her. It took everything in Adrian not to hop on that elevator right then and there.

He picked up his speed and entered the room the engineers wheeled Caesar through. It was a lab filled with large mechanical equipment. Along the far wall were three rows of identical Caesars. An army of robots. Even if he had managed to disable Caesar, they would send another one right back out.

"So his control panel was smoking?" the female engineer said.

Adrian tried to sound as calm and confident as possible. "Yes, it was smoking, so I undid the hatch, but then there was no smoke."

"So he was smoking, but he wasn't smoking?"

The second engineer said, "Did you touch anything on the motherboard?"

"No," Adrian said quickly. "I mean, it's possible I knocked something out of place, but not to my knowledge."

The engineer examined the motherboard and caught his meddling instantly. "It's the fuse. Looks like it's broken."

They all shared a look and the female one nodded.

In one swift movement, the first engineer unlatched a chip from the motherboard, and within seconds, Caesar went dark. So that was how to disable him.

The female engineer walked to the army of robots and inserted the chip into its motherboard.

It sprang to life. "Hello, I am Caesar," it said in an identical tone to the one on the cart.

"Caesar, welcome to your new body. We're going to evaluate the old model and find out what went wrong."

"Thank you, Darfur." Caesar gave a stiff bow to the engineer and walked over to Adrian. "I am eternally grateful for your help, warden. Let me escort you back to your office."

Adrian just smiled, not wanting to arouse any more suspicion among the engineers. He waved goodbye and followed Caesar out of the room.

As they approached the elevator, Adrian said, "You know, I've never had a tour of the lower levels. Would you take me on one?"

"Tours are not allowed below. Only authorized personnel can enter the site."

"What about a snack room? I'm hungry."

"That is by the entrance. But there are also snacks at your office."

The elevator doors were opening as they passed. Adrian stepped inside and caused Caesar to do a double-take.

"Warden, you are not allowed in there."

"This isn't the way out?" Adrian punched the door close button, but Caesar put his hand out and stopped them from shutting.

He stepped inside. "Evacuate at once."

Adrian widened his eyes and pointed behind the robot. "You're smoking again!"

Caesar twirled, and this time, Adrian opened the hatch and yanked the chip out of the motherboard. He hit the "door close" button as Caesar dropped to the ground.

"Going down," the elevator said.

Adrian's heart raced as he attached the drive to the motherboard and downloaded the information, the now-deactivated Caesar in a clump beside him. As the elevator descended from Floor 1 to Lower Level 2, the download bar inched along. Adrian realized he wouldn't get far in his usual form. No, the lower levels were reserved for alien personnel only. If that door opened and an alien stood on the other side, he'd be doomed whether or not they realized what he was doing. He had to try it, even if it didn't work. Even if he broke his bones and ended up crumpled on the floor like Caesar. He had to try for Anna.

Adrian shut his eyes, imagining the alien he had just met with the kind eyes. He kept her form in his mind's eye as the familiar cramping took over. Pain shot through his limbs—stronger than ever before—as they morphed and grew. His small sheep hands were replaced by long, webbed ones with nubby fingers. His torso stretched like a piece of taffy, bursting from the oxygen suit he still had on. He unzipped the suit just as his face compressed and then expanded well past what the mask would have allowed. Adrian held his breath, unsure if he was sentencing himself to death or if his new physiology would hold up in the aliens' element. His wool shed as leathery skin covered him from head to toe.

The download bar completed as the doors opened. Adrian dropped Caesar's motherboard beside him and put the drive in his pocket. He sipped in a tiny breath of air—whatever it was made of—and found he was still standing. In fact, he stood taller than ever, his clothing hanging off him like he was a coat rack. He'd be questioned in a second.

Adrian slid past Caesar and peeked into the hallway. Footsteps sounded around the corner. Adrian hit the door close button and slipped out before they closed. He looked left and right. There were doors all along the hall. He tried each one until he reached one that was unlocked.

He shut the door behind him and looked around the five-square-foot room. Cleaning supplies and boxes filled the shelves all the way to the ceiling. Even the alien lair had a janitor's closet. If Adrian was going to make it undetected, he needed to blend in. He looked around and spotted a basket of dirty clothes. He fished out one of the lab coats the engineers were wearing. There were dark brown splatters on the collar. Blood was the first thing to come to mind, but Adrian shook off the thought. It would do. He put it over his warden's uniform and cracked the door. Two aliens were walking down the hall, a bear in an oxygen suit between them with paws cuffed together. And not just any bear.

Adrian's heart rose. He took a deep breath and stepped into the hall. "Hello, excuse me."

The aliens turned around. "What do you want?"

"You're needed upstairs."

"On whose orders?"

"Jack. She said all hands on deck."

"What's going on?"

"I was just told to get you. I'll take the prisoner."

The aliens exchanged worried looks. One of them handed him a keycard. "Take him to Room Four."

"Room Four. Got it."

Adrian knew it was only a matter of minutes when they would find Caesar in the elevator. But now they wouldn't question him. They would go all the way back up and try to figure out what was going on. Still, he had to move fast.

Gregory shook under his grip. As soon as the aliens had rounded the corner he leaned in and whispered, "Where's Anna?"

The bear shot him an apprehensive look. "I don't know what you're talking about."

"Gregory, it's Adrian. I'm here to help you. But we don't have much time."

Gregory's eyes widened. "I can't believe it's you. You're a—a . . ."

Adrian nodded, uncuffing Gregory. "Do you know where Anna is?"

Gregory shook his head. "She comes and goes. She might be with the others. There are so many of us."

"Take me to them."

Gregory led Adrian down the hall, walking so fast it was practically a run. When they reached the end of the hallway, Gregory stopped in front of thick double doors.

"What now?" Adrian asked.

Gregory pointed to the card reader.

"Oh, right." Adrian swiped the card the aliens had given him and the doors slid open.

It was a cramped room, smaller than the engineer's laboratory above, with six cages jam-packed from floor to ceiling and wall to wall. Around four hybrids resided in each cage, with barely enough room for each of them to sit. All of them cowered when he entered.

Adrian took a step forward, but a rough paw clamped his arm.

"Wait!" Gregory pointed to a mask hanging on the wall—what the aliens wore. "The room is oxygenated."

"Thanks." Adrian took it and put it on before entering.

The door closed behind them.

There was a narrow walkway between the cages that Gregory started down. "It's okay, he's here to help us."

All of them stood, watching Adrian curiously. He scanned the faces in the closest cages, but none of them were Anna.

Gregory looked at Adrian expectantly.

"What?"

"What's the code?"

"What code?"

"The code to open the cages."

"I don't know."

"I thought they told you."

"Who?"

"The aliens."

"No." Adrian shrugged and looked at the keypad. It had four rows, numbers 1-9 and then *, 0, and #. There could be hundreds of possible combinations.

Adrian continued down the walkway. "Does anyone know the combination?" His voice sounded muffled and low.

Each of them cowered in turn as he passed. He realized none of them would trust him as long as he was in alien form. Adrian thought of Anna's cat form, and within seconds, was transformed. Now the mask was suffocating him. He ripped it off and revealed his new face.

"Anna?" a rabbit asked.

"Adrian, her boyfriend. Do you know where she is?"

The rabbit shook her head.

Adrian's heart sank. He was running out of time. And if Anna wasn't in here, there was a chance he wouldn't be able to find her.

An owl waddled out of the shadows. "Top left, middle right, top right, middle, middle, bottom right."

"What?"

"The code."

Adrian brought his hand to the keypad.

"Top left," the owl said again.

He punched number 1.

"Middle right."

Adrian punched 6.

"Top right . . . ," he continued to follow her instructions until the cage clicked and opened.

The occupants of the cage piled out, the owl stretching her wings wide with a sigh.

"I guess what they say about owls being wise is true," Gregory said.

"I'm not an owl," she said and transformed into a monkey. She swiftly moved to the next cage and punched in the code.

"How many of you are shapeshifters?" Adrian asked. Besides Gregory, everyone raised their hands.

Adrian helped the now-monkey open the rest of the cages and soon around twenty shapeshifters stood around him and Gregory. "There are too many of us to get out unseen, not to mention enough oxygen suits. We have to shift into aliens. We'll hide Gregory in the middle of the group."

"No way am I assuming alien form," one of them said.

"How else do you expect to get out of here alive?" said another.

"It's not right," someone else chimed in. And soon, everyone was talking over one another.

Adrian shushed them, but no one listened. He looked around in a panic, wondering if their voices could echo down the hall.

As if someone had heard him ask, the sliding doors began to open. Adrian shifted back into an alien just in time, pulling on his mask.

Everyone quieted down and stared, paralyzed, at the door.

Anna stood in the threshold, holding a keycard, hands on her hips. "What the . . ."

Adrian rushed forward to embrace her. Before he knew it, he was sailing backward, the wind knocked out of him, a shoeprint on his stomach. He gasped for air. Gregory rushed to his side.

"Anyone want to tell me what's going on here?" Anna asked.

"It's Adrian," Gregory said.

Anna's eyes widened. "Adrian?" She knelt in front of him and examined his now-alien face. "It is you. What are you doing here? You could be caught."

"Looking for you," he croaked.

Her face softened.

"We don't have much time. I'm getting you guys out of here."

"They need to shift," Adrian said, holding up his alien arm. "You too."

Everyone looked at Anna. She nodded, and in an instant, transformed into an alien form, holding her breath.

Like a water ripple, the others followed suit.

Once again Adrian pulled off his mask and opened the doors.

Gregory crouched in the middle of their group as they entered the hallway. The lights had turned from yellow to red. An alarm sounded somewhere in the distance.

Anna led the way, zig-zagging down hallways, through empty rooms, and back into hallways until they reached a room with pipes of all sizes. She walked to the far wall and unscrewed a capped-off pipe, just large enough to fit a body through.

"You're kidding," Adrian said.

"I tested it. It leads to the sewer system. About a mile in is rebel territory."

A few of them wasted no time, climbing into the pipe and disappearing. Everyone else lined up, awaiting their turn.

Adrian pulled Anna aside. "Are you okay?"

"Fine," she said.

"Have they done anything to you?"

She shook her head.

A loud bang sounded in the distance. Then a scream.

"We have to move fast." Adrian helped the remaining few people into the pipe and then turned to Anna. "You next."

She hesitated, glancing back at the door. Beyond it were pounding footsteps. "No, you," she said.

"I just found you. I'm not going until you go."

The footsteps were getting closer. Anna gripped his arm. "You have to go now!"

"I don't understand. You're coming. I did this whole mission just to get you out."

"Get me out? The mission was to get the rebels out."

"And you're a rebel. They took you and I'm here to get you back."

Anna's brows furrowed into a cross between confusion and pity. "They didn't tell you."

"Tell me what."

"Adrian, I'm on my own mission. I bartered with the aliens to take me to Jack. Convinced her I would feed her rebel information if she offered me safety. So I could help the cause from the inside."

Adrian's stomach felt as if she'd punched him in the gut again. "But—but that's what I'm doing."

"You didn't want to be warden. And I couldn't live with myself if they—if anything happened to you."

"And you think I could if something happened to you?"

Anna looked away to the door. "There's no more time. If you don't go now, we'll both be caught."

"But I'm warden."

"You're compromised. I saw what you did to Caesar in the elevator. You can't come back here."

Adrian knew she was right. He hadn't been thinking. All he had wanted to do was reach Anna. And now he had, but their reunion was nothing like he thought it would be. "I'm sorry," he said. "I'm sorry I didn't support the cause, support you. But I do now."

"Then you'll go. And let me stay."

"I can't."

Anna shut her eyes and took a deep breath. In an instant, she was a bear, lunging at him. The ground fell away. His shoulders hit the pipes and he was sliding. Sliding into darkness as the hole of light closed behind him, Anna on the other side.

Anna went from having two parents to two hundred parents, all of whom helped keep her safe and trained her to be a resistance leader.

Anna ran into Adrian at a safehouse that fronted as an Italian restaurant.

The resistance did not approve of their relationship.
Knock
Knock
But Anna promised she could keep their cause a secret.
TOP SECRET
Maybe she did too good of a job.

14

"**U**PSY DAISY!" GREGORY'S thick arms hugged Adrian's torso and pulled him up from the sewer muck. Adrian gasped for air and realized why he wasn't able to take in any. He shifted quickly back into sheep form. Gregory practically dragged him along, behind the other shadows of those he had just helped rescue, all the way back to the underground.

"We made it!" Gregory's voice cracked with relief and hope. They waited in line behind the others as, one by one, they passed through the entrance to the rebel sanctuary.

When it was their turn, Gregory hung back, realizing they couldn't both fit in at the same time.

"No, you go ahead," Adrian said in a daze.

Gregory didn't need telling twice. In one big step, he was across the threshold.

"Daddy, daddy!" he heard the twins' cries of joy. He watched from the other side of the door as Gregory was embraced by his wife and the twins. Gregory pointed at Adrian and his wife broke down in tears.

It was all too much for him. He turned around and walked back in the direction they had just come from.

. . .

Adrian wandered in the dark sewer pipe for hours. He felt caught between two worlds with nowhere to go. He couldn't go back to the prison and he didn't want to go back to the rebel underground—to face the people he thought were his friends. Who had been lying to him this whole time about Anna. Manipulating him to their own end. And for what? Now he was in danger. Anna was still in danger. And so were they.

Adrian came to a fork in the pipes. He knew the rebel prisoners had gone straight. It was another fifty feet before a ladder would take them to an opening in the sewer, where an entrance to the underground was hidden. Adrian peered down the other pipe. It was almost pitch black and he had no idea where it led. Anywhere was better than going back to those liars.

He took the unknown pipe one step at a time. His feet plopped one by one onto the shallow stream of murky water. He would walk as long as he needed to. Get as far away from everyone as possible.

Suddenly, a screeching gave way to a beam of light up ahead. One figure, then another appeared in the pipe opening and lowered with a plunk onto the pipe bottom, not ten feet from where Adrian stood. They were both short and lean with ears and tails. Mice by the looks of it.

They scuttled toward him, out of breath. "Help us!"

"They're after us!" they said simultaneously.

Adrian stood rooted to the spot. "Sorry, I've filled my Good Samaritan quota for the day."

The mice looked at one another and Adrian didn't have to guess their expressions. He sighed and pointed back the way he came. "Right at the fork and to the ladder."

"Thank you!" one of them squealed and they ran past him.

Before Adrian could decide whether to keep going, a large figure fell from the pipe opening the mice just ran from and landed in a crouch facing the opposite direction. Now he understood the mice's urgency: a masked alien rose to full height and brushed itself off.

Adrian had about ten seconds to figure out what he was going to do before it saw him. Stay in sheep form, he was as good as gone. Shift into a battle form like a dragon and he had a long laborious fight in front of him. Only one other option remained, one with a time limit.

Adrian thought again of the nice engineer and just barely transformed into her alien form before the alien in front of him turned to face him.

The alien cocked its head, pointing to its own mask.

Adrian wasn't sure how long he'd be able to hold his breath. He lunged forward, grabbing the alien's mask and yanking it down.

The alien's arms swung wildly at Adrian, but he kept his grip on the mask. Eventually, the alien clutched at its face. He was suffocating.

As Adrian felt the pressure building in his chest, he realized this alien's life was in his hands. He had never killed anyone—or anything—before in his life. Was that about to change?

No. Adrian wasn't a killer.

He let go of the alien's mask and it scrambled to secure it.

Feeling as if he was about to burst, Adrian shifted into dragon form.

"I'm sorry," Adrian said.

The alien stood dumbstruck for a moment. Then he came at Adrian full force, knocking him down with a splash. Adrian's nose filled with an overwhelming stench. He sputtered and turned over. The masked alien shook his shoulders and pushed his head into the watery grime.

Adrian grappled for the alien's mask again, but all he caught was air.

Now he really was suffocating. A mix of mucky water and webbed hands on his throat.

He was going to die here.

As he lost consciousness, a flash of warm light burst from behind the alien. He felt the pressure released from his neck, the putrid water receding. And then there was darkness again.

■ ■ ■

Adrian gasped for air and scrambled upright. His eyes flashed open to a flickering candle beside him. He was not sopping wet in a sewer but cocooned in a faded sheet on a cot. His legs and arms were not woolen or furry or even leathery, but thick and scaly.

Adrian's heart picked up speed as he realized he had shifted into his original form. Someone had saved him. And that meant someone had seen him as a dragon. And they had brought him back to the underground.

Did they know who he was?

Adrian rolled off the cot and ambled to the door. His tail swung wildly behind him, hitting the side table, which luckily was bolted into place. Upon closer look, this room was larger than the rest he had seen. As if it was made for a dragon.

Adrian latched his claw onto the door handle and twisted. It caught at half a rotation. It was locked. Someone had locked him in.

Adrian fisted his claw and banged on the door. "Hello?" His voice came out gravelly. "Hello, let me out."

Adrian looked around, but the rocky wall's curves and crevices showed no other exits. He banged on the door once more and then sat back on the cot.

He lost Anna, he was attacked by an alien, and now taken prisoner? What else could possibly go wrong?

Footsteps echoed from beyond the door.

Adrian snatched the candle from the bedside table and then realized he had plenty of fire in his belly to fight whoever was coming for him. He set the candle back down and stood in the center of the room.

The lock clicked and the doorknob twisted. The heavy metal door swung wide where two large figures were backlit.

The larger took a step into the room. "We thought we lost you there, buddy." Blood Cry gave him a toothy smile and patted his shoulder.

Adrian stiffened. "You know it's me."

"Of course I do. I've seen you as a dragon, remember? During training."

The other figure stepped forward into the light, revealing Lola. "We're so glad you're okay," she said in such a tone that he almost believed it. "We were able to recover the drive with the map. You did it, Adrian."

Adrian turned away, forgetting his tail, which made contact with Lola's leg. "I didn't want to come back here."

"What do you mean?" Lola asked.

"Because the aliens were chasing you? Don't worry, I took care of that."

Adrian spun rapidly, wincing as his tail hit the wall. "Because you're liars!"

Lola and Blood Cry both reflected the same dumbfounded expression.

"I found Anna. She helped me get everyone out. And then . . ." Adrian's voice cracked. He took a breath. "You told me we would rescue her. You told me you would do everything in your power to bring her back. But she doesn't want to leave and you guys don't want her to either. You lied to me. You lied so I would help you. Admit it!"

Blood Cry and Lola shared a knowing look.

"Adrian," Lola said carefully, "what we said was true."

Adrian scoffed, looking around wildly for another way out of the room that he already knew didn't exist.

"We will rescue her. And we will do everything in our power to bring her back. But not yet."

"How am I supposed to believe you? And it doesn't matter anyway. I'm done with Anna. I'm done with you guys. With the whole rebel cause. You can rescue her or not. I don't care anymore." He shifted into sheep form and shoved past them.

"Come on, buddy," Blood Cry said. "You don't mean that. You're one of us."

"I don't lie to get what I want. I don't play with people's lives."

"Don't you?" Lola called.

Adrian faltered.

"What would you have done if we had told you Anna didn't want to be rescued? Would you still have helped us?"

Adrian remained still, not daring to turn around or answer.

"And if we had told you before the mission, what would you have done? Compromised all of us to rescue her. You didn't have to tell me the truth for me to understand you, Adrian. I have accepted that for you we are a means to your own end. We have been very upfront about our end. It's you who have failed to accept it."

Adrian shut his eyes. She was right. He was no different than they were. But still, he felt betrayed. He didn't want to stay, but he didn't know where he would go either.

"Go if you want. But before you do, there's someone you should see."

"Who?" he asked.

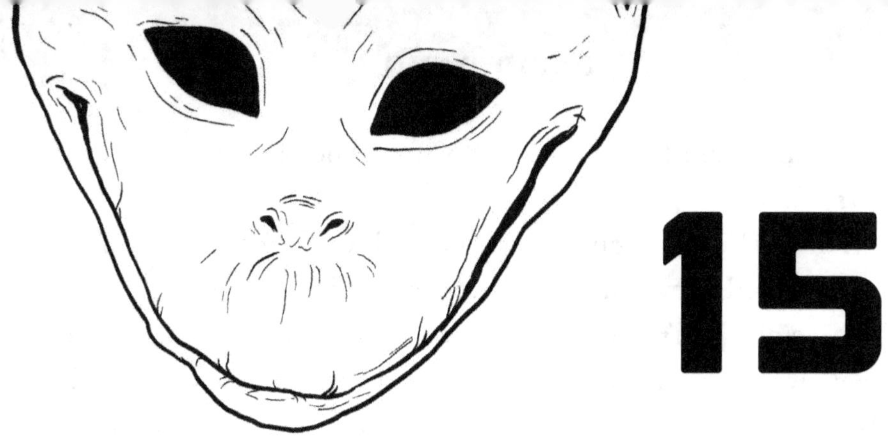

15

LOLA LED ADRIAN to the same cell he had woken up in his first time in the underground. When he didn't know any of them yet. When they weren't sure of his intentions.

The person inside was lying on the cot, facing away from them, head sunken into the pillow.

Adrian skirted around the cell, watching the body as he passed each bar until he could finally make out the familiar lizard's profile.

"Zeke!" Adrian shook the bars and turned to Lola. "Let him out."

Zeke lifted his bandaged head and winced.

"Your friend has suffered a concussion, not to mention the minor burns and lacerations. He needs rest."

"What happened? Why did you bring him here?"

"Apparently you aren't his only friend down here." Lola unlocked the cell and held the door open.

Adrian looked from Zeke to Lola. He imagined a sheep in his mind's eye and transformed into the shape Zeke knew him as. Once he stepped inside the cell, Lola shut and locked it behind him. "I'll be back."

Adrian dropped to his knees beside Zeke, his stomach knotting as he thought of the previous day's events. How he barely waved hello to Zeke. Didn't bother to tell him what was going on. He could have warned him. Could have told him to run. And then he wouldn't be hurt. Or worse.

Adrian put his hand on Zeke's. "Hi buddy. How are you feeling?"

Zeke blinked a few times. "Adrian, is that you?"

"Yes, it's me. You're safe now. Do you remember what happened?"

"There was a fire. I called the fire department, but it was spreading fast. The prisoners were panicking. I came to find you, but you weren't in your office. When I went back, someone was letting them out of their cages. Lots of someones. I recognized one of them—Georgina. You know, from Georgina's Cantina."

Adrian nodded, unable to speak. If he had only been honest with Zeke from the beginning.

Zeke continued. "There was no time to ask questions. The fire was so close. I helped her get more prisoners out, but a few of them saw my uniform and attacked. It's all a blur after that."

"I'm so sorry," Adrian squeaked.

Zeke pushed himself up.

Adrian turned the pillow vertically and fluffed it up behind him so he could lean back.

"Where were you?" Zeke asked.

Adrian opened and shut his mouth. If he told his friend the truth, he would never forgive him. But if he lied, he was no better than the people who betrayed him.

"I wanted to tell you as soon as it happened," Adrian started. "Anna was captured at the rally—or she wanted to be. And then the rebels took me. They told me if I helped them they would help me save Anna. They told me I couldn't tell anyone. I wanted to."

"Whoa, slow down. You told me Anna was visiting her cousin."

"I didn't want you to get involved. I thought I was keeping you safe."

"Where's Anna, Adrian?"

Adrian shut his eyes and took a deep breath. And when he let it out, he told Zeke everything. About the rebels. About Anna's plan. About everything he'd done for the rebellion and to try and get her back. And how she didn't want to be rescued. About how he'd been betrayed. And how as soon as Zeke was better, he would get them out of there. Leave it all behind.

Zeke listened in silence, at one point lowering back down to rest.

When Adrian finally finished, Zeke remained silent, staring at the ceiling.

"Please say something."

"You've been a bad friend," Zeke said.

Adrian's chest tightened. He nodded. "I know. I didn't want to get caught up in any of this. I knew it was dangerous and I knew you wouldn't approve. I thought it was the only way to save Anna and it turns out, it was all for nothing."

"Nothing?" Zeke struggled to push himself up again, but winced, bringing a hand to his head.

Adrian reached out to brace him, but Zeke swatted him away. He managed to sit up the rest of the way. "If you had told me what happened, you think I would have thrown you in a jail cell?"

Adrian shrugged.

"You think I'm on the aliens' side and would be perfectly happy with them fully taking over?"

Adrian didn't bother to reply to that, feeling foolish for ever doubting his friend.

Zeke continued. "You've always been concerned with your own life; I know that. But if you had bothered to ask whose side I was on, I would have told you it's the side of freedom."

"You mean, you'd help the rebels?"

"I was a man of the law before the aliens came. I follow their rules, sure. But you think I want to see my friends behind bars? You think I don't know what they do to our people in their lair?"

Now Adrian remained silent, dumbfounded by his friend's beliefs.

"And now that Anna didn't want to abandon her mission, you want to run away. That's always been the plan for you, hasn't it?"

"I'm just trying to protect the people I love."

"If you leave, you aren't protecting anyone but yourself."

"So after everything. After I lied and put you in danger, after the rebels attacked you, you're still going to stay here?"

"This isn't about you and me. This isn't about Anna or even the rebels. This is about the greater good. I am mad at you. But that doesn't mean you aren't worth fighting for."

Zeke extended a bandaged hand toward Adrian.

A lump formed in Adrian's throat as he took it, speechless.

"Now where's the rebel leader? I have some vital information for the next attack."

ADRIAN, ZEKE, AND Blood Cry sat in the cafeteria eating the usual porridge.

"Looks like your cuts have healed enough to begin training," Blood Cry said to Zeke.

Zeke ran a hand over his banged up arm. "You think so?"

"We can still take it easy. You can watch me and Adrian and then join in when you feel like it."

Adrian suddenly wasn't very hungry. Zeke was going to *watch* him train. That meant he would see him shift. Another secret he had kept from his friend.

"I think you should get more rest," Adrian said.

"I can rest and watch at the same time." Zeke elbowed him gently and then winced. "Definitely no contact," he added and even Adrian had to laugh.

• • •

Adrian stood at the center of the training room, Blood Cry across from him. Zeke lounged on some pillows in the corner.

"Watch carefully, Zeke," Blood Cry called. "You're going to learn this in due time."

Not exactly, Adrian wanted to say. Because Zeke was not a shapeshifter. He couldn't believe Blood Cry didn't understand this was a big deal for him. That maybe he wanted to tell his friend on his own terms.

"All right, let's do dragon," Blood Cry said.

Adrian stared wide-eyed at Blood Cry. Really? His original form? He shook his head.

"Okay, how about cat?"

Adrian glanced at Zeke. He watched the two of them good-naturedly, an innocent smile on his face.

"Let's just start," Adrian said, adopting a fighting stance.

Blood Cry let out a breath. "We train for a reason, Adrian. You could have shifted out of that situation in the sewer. Instead, you lost control."

Adrian felt his cheeks grow hot. He glanced at Zeke, then at the ground.

Blood Cry sighed. "He's going to find out one way or another."

Now Zeke perked up. "Find out what?"

Blood Cry cocked a hand on his hip. "It's really not a big deal."

"Maybe not to you," Adrian snapped.

"What's not a big deal?" Now Zeke was standing, hobbling on his good foot.

Adrian shut his eyes. "I told you no more secrets."

Adrian imagined his original form and felt tingling in his limbs. Once he'd shifted into a dragon he imagined a cat. Then a rabbit. Then a horse. Each shift he paused long enough for Zeke to see until he was back to the form Zeke knew him as since they were kids. He stood there as a sheep, panting, his whole body shaking—not from the effort, but from the vulnerability.

Zeke lowered back to the ground, his mouth agape.

"I understand if you never want to talk to me again," he said.

Zeke opened and shut his mouth a few times, then swallowed. "This makes so much more sense."

"It does?"

"Why you're so guarded. Why you never want to be in anyone's way. Why you wanted to run. You could have told me. I would have . . ."

Zeke trailed off. And in that moment something unspoken ran between them. Zeke understood why Adrian had to keep it a secret. And Zeke wouldn't have been able to do anything for him other than know a secret dangerous enough to get him killed or imprisoned.

"I'm sorry," Adrian said anyway.

"I am too," Zeke said.

"Okay then." Blood Cry clapped his hands together. "Can we get back to training then?"

■ ■ ■

After training, Adrian went with Zeke to meet with Lola. She was in her office, looking over a blueprint.

"I see you got my message," Zeke said, gesturing to the blueprint.

"So you're telling me there's an underground armory below the prison?"

"They converted a basement into a weapons room. I'm the only guard who knows about it. And I still have the key." He held up a rusty skeleton key.

"Zeke and I can go tonight," Adrian said. "The sooner we have those weapons, the better."

"It's too risky. The aliens are on guard now after our breakout. I wish we'd known about this before our attack . . ."

Adrian and Zeke shared a look. If only Adrian had confided in Zeke sooner.

"We won't have to go above ground at all," Zeke added. "We can take the sewer pipes all the way to the room."

"Fine. But you'll take a team. Blood Cry. And Fiona."

"Fiona?" The name sounded familiar to Adrian.

"Fiona Whiskers. She worked at Robotics Inc. before the aliens came."

Adrian's stomach did a flip. He remembered this woman from the night they planned the prison breakout. She'd asked what Caesar's model number was. Anna had taken the identity of a real person. He wondered if Fiona knew.

• • •

The team of four gathered at the sewer's entrance just before midnight.

"Zeke, Adrian, this is Fiona Whiskers," Blood Cry said.

Zeke stuck his hand out. "Pleasure to meet you."

She smiled and shook his hand. Then turned to Adrian. "Hi again."

"Hi," Adrian managed, not wanting to say too much.

Blood Cry opened the sewer and the four of them went through.

"I'm glad the mission went well with Caesar," she said, stepping in stride with Adrian.

"What? Oh yeah, mostly."

"Thanks for letting me come along tonight."

"Lola's orders," Adrian said.

"Right." She sounded somewhat disappointed.

"I could have used your expertise during the break-in. I'm sure you would have deactivated Caesar without the mess I caused."

"Well, you got everyone out. That's what matters."

"Not everyone," Adrian mumbled, his heart aching as he thought of Anna.

Fiona placed her hand gently on his shoulder. "She'll come back to you," she said.

"You can't know that," Adrian said.

Fiona removed her hand.

The sewer grew silent but for the sludging of their feet in the muck below.

After a while, Fiona sighed. "What I wouldn't give to see their engineering labs. Did either of you see it?"

"Not me," Zeke said. "Alien lair was off-limits to most of us."

"I did, the day of the attack," Adrian said. "They were trying to fix Caesar after I pulled the fuse."

"Let's keep quiet, folks," Blood Cry said. "Don't know what could be waiting on the other side of the door."

Adrian was shocked to find they were already approaching the ladder leading up to the armory.

Zeke walked a few paces ahead of them and turned to face them. "Okay. As soon as I open the door, we each fill our bags as high as possible. It doesn't matter if we get it all. Just take what you can and get out, okay?"

Adrian nodded along with the others.

Zeke climbed the ladder first, putting his ear to the hatch above. Footsteps echoed on the ceiling. Zeke's hand shot to his mouth for them to stay quiet. There were muffled voices above. Adrian felt like he held his breath for an hour before the footsteps and voices retreated.

Zeke put his ear to the hatch again and nodded. Then he turned the key in the lock and opened the hatch. Fiona followed after him, then Blood Cry, and finally Adrian.

The room was cold, with gray steel cabinets from top to bottom. Cabinets with locks.

"You have more keys, right?" Adrian asked.

"Usually the keys are in the locks," Zeke said. "They must have taken them out in case."

"In case of this?" Blood Cry said, letting out a frustrated exhale.

Fiona extended one of her claws and attempted to jam it into the closest keyhole.

Adrian pinched his eyes shut. He had done it before. He could do it again.

He put his hand on Fiona's shoulder. "I can."

She stepped aside as he placed his finger above the keyhole and imagined his finger molding to the unique lock within. His finger slid through the gap and felt a click when he turned it. The cabinet creaked open to reveal an array of rifles.

"This one next." Zeke pointed to a cabinet across the way while Blood Cry filled his bag.

Once it was open, Zeke moved in to fill his bag, and Adrian moved on to the next one.

"Jackpot," Blood Cry breathed as the next cabinet revealed three laser guns.

"No pun intended," Zeke said.

Adrian looked around for Fiona, who was mere inches from the main door leading up to the prison.

"Fiona, what are you doing?"

Zeke and Blood Cry turned their attention to her too.

"I need you to open the door, Adrian," she said.

"What? No. We're supposed to get the weapons and leave."

"You are. I'm not."

Adrian looked to Blood Cry, who seemed just as surprised as him and Zeke.

"I have to get Caesar. Zeke, does your key work?"

Zeke took a step toward her. "If you go out there and get caught . . ."

"I won't," she said matter-of-factly. "Give me ten minutes."

The three of them exchanged glances.

"It's not worth the risk," Zeke said.

"It might be," Blood Cry sighed. He held his hand out for the key and Zeke obliged.

"Ten minutes," Blood Cry said. "Not a minute longer. If he's not out there—"

"Got it," she said, slipping through the door as soon as it opened.

Blood Cry shut it behind her.

"You didn't know about this?" Adrian asked.

Blood Cry shook his head. "Sometimes Lola thinks the less people who know the real plan the better."

"That hasn't worked out for me so far," Adrian mumbled as he began to fill his bag with Glock handguns and bullets.

He opened one more cabinet so Blood Cry and Zeke could fill Fiona's bag.

The minutes dragged by like whole days. Once he'd filled his bag, Adrian kept his eyes on the door and listened for Fiona.

"That's ten minutes," Blood Cry said, tying up his bag.

"We're just going to leave her?" Zeke asked, walking toward the door.

Adrian grabbed his arm. "She knew the risk."

Blood Cry tossed Zeke the key. "Lock the door."

Zeke hesitated. Blood Cry was already climbing his way back down the ladder.

Adrian rushed forward and put his finger to the lock. Just as his finger began to transform, the door pushed open.

Fiona burst in and shoved the door shut behind her.

"Thank God!" Now Zeke came forward and locked the door.

The three of them made their way down the ladder. Zeke closed and locked the hatch behind him. They plopped onto the sewer muck and hoisted the bags over their shoulders.

Blood Cry held Fiona's bag out to her. "No luck getting Caesar, huh?"

But Fiona didn't take the bag. Her gaze was fixed on Adrian. She leaned toward him and pressed her lips against his.

Adrian froze, unsure what to do. He let her kiss him and when she pulled away, it wasn't Fiona he was staring at, but Anna.

"I'm sorry," she said. "For everything."

17

BLOOD CRY MADE them keep quiet for the rest of the journey back to the underground, which wasn't hard considering they were each lugging fifty pounds of guns and ammunition on their backs.

Adrian was in shock. Anna, his Anna, who refused to leave the alien lair with him just a couple weeks ago, was now right beside him. It made no sense—why would Fiona want to stay? Why had Anna taken on her identity in the first place? Unless all of it had been planned all along.

Lola was waiting for them when they arrived. She and Anna embraced like mother and daughter reunited after a long trip away.

"So the plan was successful," Lola said as she and Anna untangled themselves.

"Well, yes, but—"

"The plan?" Adrian interjected. "Fiona knew she was going to stay there?"

"She's the only one who can truly sabotage the aliens' technology. We couldn't afford to wait any longer."

"Why all the secrets? If that was a rescue mission and not an armory break-in, why not just tell us?"

"It was both," Lola said. "We couldn't have the three of you waiting around if something went wrong."

Even Blood Cry appeared shocked by the turn of events. He leaned against the wall, eyes fixed on Lola.

"I said if I stayed, no more secrets. No more betrayals."

"Adrian, this isn't about you," Anna huffed. "If everyone knew everything we would have been compromised a long time ago."

"This isn't about me? Well, it's clearly about you."

"What's that supposed to mean?"

"You and Lola clearly don't have any regard for anything but the greater good, no matter whom it harms in the process."

"How could you think that?"

Adrian leaned in and lowered his voice, looking Anna up and down. "You took someone's identity. We promised never to do that. The first rule of shapeshifting."

"The rules don't apply anymore. In case you didn't notice, the rules are being rewritten as we speak."

"Let's all just calm down," Lola said. "We can talk this all through later. But right now Anna really needs to be debriefed after three months with the aliens."

"Go ahead. Tell more secrets." Adrian stormed down the hallway. When he reached the split in the tunnels, voices echoed around him. Screams.

He couldn't make them out, but they were clearly panicked. He turned around to find Lola, Blood Cry, Anna, and Zeke rushing toward him, all of them armed.

The screams came again. This time it was clear which tunnel they were from. They started down it. The screams grew louder. Adrian finally made out one word clearly: "Aliens!"

His heart raced, not just from running. He had a very bad feeling.

Footsteps sounded from the other end of the tunnel. A flood of people headed their way.

"They've broken in!" one of them shouted.

"Infiltrated," said another.

"The aliens are here!"

Blood Cry moved in front of them and put out his arms. Adrian slowed along with the others while the undergrounders rushed past.

"This—" Anna panted. "What—I—trying—to tell . . ."

"What— is it?" Lola asked.

Anna stood upright and took a deep breath in. "The serum worked. They can breathe in our atmosphere. It's over."

# 18

MORE AND MORE people stampeded down the hallway toward their group.

"Code red," Lola said. "We have to get them out of here."

"And go where? We haven't planned for an underground attack," Blood Cry said.

"I know," Zeke said. "There's a place in the prison. Completely fortified. If we can get everyone there, the aliens won't be able to reach us. If someone has a map, I should be able to navigate underground for most of the way."

"You want to take everyone we just freed back to prison?" Blood Cry asked.

"I know it sounds crazy, but what part of this isn't?"

Blood Cry shook his head but said no more.

Lola stepped forward. "Anna, Blood Cry—you head them off. I'll hang back to guide people in the right direction. Zeke, let's get you a map."

"I'm coming too," Adrian said.

Lola and Blood Cry exchanged a look.

"He's ready," Blood Cry said.

Lola nodded but pulled Adrian aside. "I was hoping there would be more time, but there's no telling what's going to happen. You need to protect that watch at all costs. It's the key to disabling the energy source. I just don't know how yet."

Adrian instinctively grabbed his wrist wearing the watch. "What?"

"Come on, dude," Blood Cry summoned Adrian forward.

"Go," Lola said breathlessly. So he did.

Adrian, Anna, and Blood Cry ran side by side, the weapons they had just stolen from the armory slung across their backs. Anna had started out behind them and was now three paces in front of them and counting.

"Wait—for—us," Adrian panted, anger mixing with his anxiety at how reckless Anna was being—how reckless she had been this whole time without him knowing.

Blood Cry signaled Adrian to slow as they drew closer to the infiltrated door. Only a few stragglers were running past them now.

Several bodies lay lifeless on the floor and Adrian forced himself not to look down.

As they rounded the corner, Anna was already in position, laser gun pointed at three aliens—mask-less aliens—who seemed much taller in the confines of the cave walls.

"Not another step closer," she said and fired the laser gun just left of one of the alien's heads. As soon as it fired, the gun jolted out of Anna's hands and skidded into the wall.

The aliens exchanged satisfied glances, and in an instant, one of them swooped in and grabbed Anna.

Adrian's heart lurched. He had just gotten her back.

Blood Cry stepped in front of Adrian, full knowing he might have done something stupid on instinct.

Adrian watched Anna struggle against the alien's grasp. The other two pointed their guns at him and Blood Cry.

"On my signal," Blood Cry said in an even tone, raising his fist. "One, two, . . ." He put up the three fingers that meant dragon. He wanted to fight fire with fire.

"No!" Adrian said before Blood Cry could say three. "It's too dangerous."

"Do it, Adrian!" Anna shouted.

"I'm not risking losing you again."

"You have to trust us," she said.

Blood Cry rounded on Adrian, a fire behind his eyes he'd never seen. "One, two, . . ."

On three, Adrian shut his eyes and shifted into a dragon. Red and orange lit up under his eyelids and heat licked his face. Blood Cry had already let loose his fire breath.

An instant later, Adrian opened his eyes in dragon form. Blood Cry had moved forward, still spewing flames at the aliens.

Adrian looked around wildly for Anna, but she was no longer in their clutches. She too had transformed into a dragon and was helping Blood Cry guide the aliens back out the door with her fire breath. Adrian rushed forward and inhaled until he felt the warm rumble in his belly. He stepped between Anna and Blood Cry and let out his fire breath to combine with theirs. The aliens covered their faces, one of them giving up and running back out the door. Just as Adrian thought his breath would give out, the other two went through as well.

Blood Cry lunged forward and locked the door.

The three of them stood there, panting, leftover embers glowing around them.

"You did good, kid," Blood Cry said to him.

"I'm sorry I—I didn't realize Anna would . . ."

Anna transformed back into dog form and took his hands. "I haven't been trying to lie to you or keep things from you. I've been trying to protect you."

"All I've wanted is to protect you. And you make it so hard."

Blood Cry interjected. "I think it's safe to say neither one of you needs protecting anymore. He looked in the direction of the door. "Now, I have a feeling that wasn't the last of them today."

"Zeke," Adrian said, and they all took off back in the direction they came.

●　●　●

By the time they reached Lola, Adrian was out of breath. He, Anna, and Blood Cry wove in and out of the panicking rebels. Lola stood at the base of the ladder leading them above ground. One by one, they climbed the ladder.

"Please form a single-file line," Lola called and by her tone, it seemed this was not the first time. "Everyone will make it to safety, but we have to work together—"

Her voice was drowned out by the zipping of a laser gun being fired, followed by a ripple of screams. Footsteps pummeled the ground above them.

Lola halted the next rebel and beckoned Blood Cry, Adrian, and Anna over. "Zeke's alone up there," she said.

Anna grabbed a few rounds of ammo from one of the bags they'd filled and threw them to Adrian. He didn't wait for them before ascending the ladder.

Once above, the scene was pure chaos. Rebels ran in every direction. At least fifty aliens, all armed with laser guns, shot at them from a safe distance. Half of them were mask-less. Clearly there wasn't yet enough serum to go around—their only advantage.

Zeke stood in the middle of it all, gesturing as many people as he could toward what used to be the polar bear enclosure, about a football field's distance away. It was genius—the enclosure had caves and was made of glass no laser or bullets could penetrate. They just had to get there.

Adrian looked around wildly for some sort of protection. A few feet away, a trash can lid wheeled to a circular halt. Adrian grabbed it and held it like a shield in front of him, running through the crowd toward Zeke.

Anna and Blood Cry darted from the underground's entrance, circling around the crowd toward the aliens.

Adrian reached Zeke and put up the shield in front of them.

"Adrian, thank goodness!"

"I'm getting you out of here," he said.

Zeke gave him a confused look. "But we have to get them out of here." He pointed to the closest rebel.

Adrian looked around and noticed that the closer everyone got to Zeke, the more organized they became. People ran single-file toward the enclosure.

At the front lines, Blood Cry used his fire breath against the aliens. Those with masks on were unaffected, but the unmasked ones recoiled and coughed as the smoke engulfed them. Anna twisted and jumped, transforming from one shape to another as she disarmed one, two, then three aliens. She threw a laser gun to Blood Cry and looked around wildly, clearly looking for him.

"Okay, I'll be right back," Adrian said. "Take this." He pressed the makeshift shield into Zeke's hands and took off toward Anna.

Relief showed clearly on her face as she spotted him and threw him a laser gun.

"We've got to hold them off," she yelled, shooting at an approaching alien.

Adrian moved forward, taking Anna's cue and changing form every so often to make himself a harder target. With each new form, he shot the laser at an alien. His stomach leapt as one went down. They could do this.

Adrian shifted to a dragon and summoned the fire in his belly. He stood beside Blood Cry and directed the fire toward the closest alien. It dropped in an instant, flailing on the ground surrounded by flames. Adrian pinched his eyes shut for a moment, hoping all of this was a dream.

Adrian shifted into a rabbit, making sure to keep his choices varied in size. Sure enough, a laser shot just above his ears.

Behind him, Zeke appeared to have the crowd under control. And it was nearly half the size it had been moments ago. Adrian felt his nerves settling. They could do this. Everything would be okay.

Lola appeared at the top of the ladder, guiding the last few rebels toward Zeke. A gun was slung across her back.

An alien spotted her and tipped off his group so all of them turned their attention toward her. In unison, they lifted their laser guns and pointed them at her moving form.

"Anna, look," Adrian called, but she was already running toward Lola.

Adrian and Blood Cry shot at the aliens, as one began tracking Anna with his weapon.

Adrian's blood ran thin. "Anna!" He took off after her, but she was at least ten feet ahead.

Lola's eyes widened as she registered the line of aliens and Anna running toward her. She shoved the rebels toward Zeke, who threw her the trashcan shield just as the aliens fired.

A barrage of laser beams hit the lid, deflecting in twenty different directions as the lid hurtled at lightning speed past Lola.

It was as if all the sound had been sucked out of the world.

Adrian held his breath as the smoky residue cleared.

Lola remained standing, unscathed.

Anna had stopped mid-run, unable to see past the smoke.

Blood Cry too stood paralyzed.

Zeke was no longer where Adrian had clocked him moments ago. He looked at the remaining rebels who were almost to the polar bear enclosure. But he wasn't with them.

A burning, rotten smell filled the air.

Without thinking, Adrian ran forward, and through the debris, found his friend.

Adrian's heart seized momentarily.

Zeke was lying on his side, a gaping black hole across his back. Smoke lingered on the singed edges of his shirt.

"Zeke!" Adrian rolled him onto his back. His eyes stared at nothing, his mouth half open. No breath came from it.

His dearest friend in the world was gone.

19

ADRIAN COULDN'T TAKE his eyes off of Zeke. He was aware of Anna shouting for him to move as she shot at the aliens. Of Lola leading the remaining rebels to the enclosure. And then of Blood Cry hoisting him to his feet.

Adrian jerked away. "I'm not leaving him!"

He bent back down and scooped his arms under Zeke's. He lifted but could barely scoot him an inch.

"Help me," he said, shifting into gorilla form so he had more strength.

Anna continued to shoot at the aliens. "You gotta move now," she shouted.

Blood Cry grunted and rushed to lift Zeke's bottom half. Together they carried him several feet. Adrian's heart rose; they would make it.

Anna tracked their progress and covered them, just barely managing to deflect the lasers away from their group.

Suddenly, the aliens stopped attacking.

Adrian couldn't help but slow his pace. Blood Cry too looked around, confused.

And then they heard it. A low hum in the distance.

Above the buildings, a small alien craft sped toward them.

"Run!" Blood Cry shouted, dropping Zeke's feet.

The aliens lowered their weapons and moved to form a half-circle barrier. For what? Or whom?

Adrian stood rooted to the spot as the craft landed just behind them and none other than Jack exited. She too was unmasked.

Adrian's legs shook, but he knew the time for running had passed. It was time to stand his ground and confront Jack. He gently lowered Zeke's body to the ground and did what he never thought he would do in public, let alone in front of the alien leader. He shifted back into the sheep form she knew him as. Jack's eyes roamed over him as he transformed.

"I did have my suspicions," she said. "But I must say I'm very disappointed, Adrian."

"Why are you doing this, Jack?" he asked. "The imprisonment, the killing. Enough people have died for you. Let us go."

"Let you go? Let you *go*. That is precisely what I aimed to do when we first touched down upon this planet. But it quickly became clear that your kind takes for granted what you have. If I had let you all run around freely for much longer, this planet wouldn't be inhabitable for anyone."

"Then we can work together to make it better."

"Together? I chose you as warden because that's precisely what I had in mind. You appeared to be the one person who would follow my orders and not ask questions. Who would set an example to the others: obey and no harm will come. That was all I asked of all of you. But now look where we are."

Adrian's stomach churned. She was right. Adrian always followed orders blindly, didn't ask questions. If Anna hadn't been fighting for the rebel cause, he wouldn't have ever gone against Jack. Then where would they be?

"What do you want from us now?" Adrian asked. "What would you have us do?"

"Adrian," Anna hissed. "What are you doing?"

"Now?" Jack lifted her arms and the army around her lifted their guns. "I would have you all die."

"Run!" Blood Cry shouted.

Anna clutched Adrian's arm and pulled him forward without hesitation. The entrance to the polar bear enclosure came into sharp focus. Lola stood at the opening, staring apprehensively past them as the whiz and flash of lasers went off all around them.

"Ah!" Blood Cry let out a painful cry. His left leg dipped and he nearly fell.

Anna let go of Adrian and each of them grabbed one of Blood Cry's arms, nearly dragging him through the door.

Lola pulled it shut and locked the hatch. The lasers continued to go off on the other side.

■　■　■

The adrenaline in Adrian's body finally subsided once he and Anna had reached the caves with Blood Cry. Lola went right to work tending to his laser wound.

Adrian found himself collapsed on his knees. His breath came in ragged spurts, meshing with the cries, coughs, and shouts from the other rebels.

Jack had backed them into a corner, like catching a spider in a jar. But they wouldn't be kindly placed outside in the dirt. They would be annihilated.

Anna was still on her feet. She rotated in a circle, arms crossed as she took in the situation. "This is much worse than I thought."

Out the windows, drones continued to circle, their whizzing lasers bouncing off the glass.

Adrian pushed himself to his feet. "She has us right where she wants us. We're done for."

One of the rebels closest to them started crying even harder.

Anna pulled him away. "We're going to get through this."

"You don't know that. This whole cause has been operated on false hope. Our parents started it and look what good it did them. Zeke had more hope than any of us and now he's—" Adrian sucked in a breath, trying not to cry as he thought of Zeke, still lying out there all alone. Adrian had given him the shield. It was his fault he was dead.

Anna grabbed Adrian's hand and held it in front of him so he could see the watch his father had left him—the only thing he had to remember them by. "Our parents understood that this was bigger than them. That they were leaving a legacy for us to continue. To fight for freedom, not just for us, but everyone who comes after."

"Look around you, Anna. No one is coming after."

Anna stared at him silently for what felt like an eternity. Blood Cry's wails echoed in the cave. "Anna," Lola called.

"I don't know who you are anymore," Anna said, before brushing past him to help Lola.

Adrian wandered further into the cave, putting as much distance as he could between him and everyone else. It was pointless. All of it.

He slumped against a stalagmite and stared at his hands. His father's watch seemed to grow heavier on his wrist.

He unlatched it and flung it onto the ground. It slid along the rocky floor and hit the opposite wall.

The dark space was suddenly lit up with an orb-like light projecting from the face of the watch. It emanated a greenish glow, hovering and spinning slowly. Adrian watched it, mesmerized. What was happening here?

He stood and approached the orb, stepping carefully forward, like approaching a wild animal. With each step, the orb seemed to grow larger. When he was finally face to face with it, it had grown to his same height.

A gentle hum emanated from the light. As it reached his ears, it almost seemed to say his name, "Addriaaaannnn." He listened harder. This time, he was sure it was his name. And it sounded like his mother's voice. "Adriaaannn," it called again.

A serene calm came over him. He was not afraid of the orb. He was not afraid of anything. Without another thought, he stepped inside.

Long ago when two solar systems were one, the planets fought to wield the power of the one sun.

Day in day out they fought for the closest position to the sun.

Round and round they went with no resolution.

Eventually, life was destroyed on all but two planets.

Life continued to dwindle on both planets until it became clear there would be no winner.

Finally both planets decided to ask for help.
We want to win
But we dont want to die.
We want to win too
Us either.
It was then that Madame Universe appeared, a starry face behind the sun.
She split the sun in two. Then the planets, each half following one of the glowing suns.
Soon life returned to every planet.
Everyone had won thanks to Madame Universe.

20

IT WAS LIKE passing through the barrier of a snow globe. Hazy, swirling fog gave way to a huge domed space. All around him was space—stars, planets, asteroids—all slowly orbiting. Beneath him was thankfully solid ground. A long, wide staircase laid before him that seemed to extend forever. He began to descend it, listening again for his mother's voice.

But all was silent.

"Hello?" he said. The word seemed to disappear as soon as he said it, unheard by anyone or anything.

He looked down at his hands and realized he was back in his dragon form. He drew a deep, warm breath and exhaled fire, lighting up the space immediately around him. A signpost made of a shimmering, silvery material lit up. Adrian had to draw another fire breath to see the words:

She is all-seeing and all-knowing.
She is all around us.
If you seek her advice,
All you must do is ask.

"Who is she?" Adrian wondered to himself.

He looked behind him and found the staircase also extended forever in that direction. He had no idea how he would get out of this place, wherever he was.

"Uh, okay," he said. "I'm asking for uh—"

He scratched his head and realized he didn't know exactly who or what to ask for.

He read the sign again.

"I'm asking for your advice. If you're all-seeing and all-knowing and all around me, then show yourself!"

Adrian waited. And waited—and waited. But nothing happened.

He paced back and forth on the staircase that somehow resembled more of a plank now.

"I give up!" he said. "I was stuck out there in a prison about to be obliterated by aliens. And now I'm stuck in here, all alone with no way out. One prison to another." He threw his hands up. "What am I supposed to do now?"

"I thought you'd never ask," said a voice that reverberated all around the space, seemingly coming from every direction.

"Who's there?" Adrian asked.

A cluster of stars above him shifted position in the sky. A figure emerged, floating down to meet him at the pace of the spinning planets beyond.

It was a woman. Or what appeared to be a woman. But she was glistening like stars, her shimmering cloak spiraling with a mirror image of the galaxies above. She spoke again, this time her voice only emitting from right before him. "I am Madame Universe."

"B—but you're just a rumor." He scanned her starry figure, sure she was an illusion. He was asleep, that was it. If he could just wake up—he pinched his arm. But still, there she was.

She turned away from him, staring at the skyscape. "A rumor begins with a grain of the truth."

"My parents, they told me stories about you when I was little. They talked as if they met you. But they were making it up."

"Were they?"

Adrian's heart quickened its pace. His mouth grew dry. He swallowed and asked the question he may have already known the answer to. "Did you know my parents?"

"I know everyone. The question should be: Did your parents know me?"

Adrian waited, but Madame Universe said no more. She just stood serenely, watching the sky as if the stars were her children, laughing and playing on a playground.

He couldn't take it any longer. "Well, did they?"

"Did they what?"

"Did my parents know you?"

"Of course they did," she said without missing a beat.

Now Adrian's heart seemed to stop completely. All this time, he thought they had been lying. Telling him stories to shield him from the big bad world. But if it was all true . . .

"My parents died because of you," he shouted. "They followed you blindly. They did everything you told them to. And it got them killed!"

Finally, Madame Universe turned back to him, her expression neutral. "Child, you are attributing power to me that I do not have. Your parents did not follow me; they followed their hearts. I offered my advice, but I did not order them to do anything. And lastly, your parents did not die because of me, because they did not die."

Now Adrian felt as if his head was the only thing spinning. He wavered where he stood, clutching his head with his hands. "But I saw their bodies. We had a funeral."

"Bodies." She waved a glimmery hand. "A technicality. We are not our bodies. We are not our minds. We just are. If you'd like to see them, I can call them here."

She said it like it was as easy as picking up the phone.

Adrian steadied himself, his heart finally slowing. "You can bring my parents back?"

"Back, no. Here, yes."

For a moment he could do nothing but stare at her.

She tilted her head. "Well? A simple nod of the head will do."

Adrian nodded.

And right before his eyes, in barely a blink, his parents glitched into existence like a digital hologram. They looked exactly the same as the last time he saw them, on the day they died. His dad in jeans and a button-up shirt, his mom in a floral skirt and white T-shirt. They were nearly the same age as him, both in their native dragon form as well.

"Mom? Dad?" Adrian held his hand out. Both of them reached for it, and when they made contact their hands were solid, warm. Like he remembered. "You're really here."

"Of course we are," his dad said. "Where else would we be?"

His mom's hand grazed his face. "It's so good to see you, honey. You're all grown up."

"The day you—the last day I saw you," Adrian said. "Did you know you were going to die?"

His parents exchanged a look before his dad spoke. "We knew it was a possibility. But no. We were certain we could win."

"You left me all alone. Both of you. One of you could have stayed."

"We had a plan to do it together."

"But your plan didn't work. It failed and you died. For nothing."

"Who said our plan didn't work?" his mom asked.

21

ADRIAN RUSHED BACK to the front of the cave where all the rebels were gathered. Blood Cry slumped against the wall, his leg now bandaged. Anna and Lola stood in a corner talking fervently below the anxious cries of the rebels and the whizzing drones and lasers on the other side of the glass. Adrian noticed the windows were starting to crack.

Blood Cry spotted him first and perked up.

Adrian halted before him, catching his breath. "I—know how—to stop them."

"What?"

Lola and Anna came over from the corner. "What's going on?" Lola asked.

Anna stood silently, her arms crossed.

"I'm sorry," he said mostly to her. "You were right. I thought our parents were crazy for fighting. I thought they blindly went into battle. But they didn't." Adrian held up his watch and looked to Lola. "What you said earlier, I know how to use it—"

Suddenly, the window shattered. Everyone scrambled away from him, screaming and shouting as drones entered.

Blood Cry held out his arm and Adrian helped him stand. He began shooting down the drones, one by one, but more kept coming. Shooting them wasn't going to stop them quickly enough.

"Fiona," Adrian shouted. "Can we contact Fiona?"

"I already have," Lola said. "It's a matter of time."

Adrian joined Anna and Blood Cry, trying to shoot the drones down as the rebels ran in every direction, some falling and diving as they were hit.

"We need to run," Adrian shouted above the noise.

"You always want to run," Anna said.

"No, I mean, we need to gather all the shapeshifters. Shift into aliens. And run into their army. They won't be able to tell us apart."

Anna stopped shooting for a moment. "That's brilliant."

Anna called out name after name of the shapeshifters in the room, all of whom did their best to navigate over to them while dodging drones and lasers. Adrian moved to Anna's other side and leaned in toward Lola as they continued to shoot at the drones. "I know how to stop them. I need a clear line into the lair."

Lola nodded, pride in her eyes. "We'll do our part."

Blood Cry continued to shoot. "I'll hold them off as long as possible," he said.

Adrian and Anna shared a look of genuine hope.

"Listen up," she shouted at the gathered crowd. "On the count of three, Adrian and I are going to open this door and all of us are going to run back outside. Set your sights on an alien and shift into that form. Do your best to stay mingled with them. Take their weapons if you can. Anything to confuse them as to who to shoot."

Adrian stood on one side of the door as Anna counted from the other. "One." He knew exactly which alien he was going to shift into. "Two." He took a deep breath and imagined her in his mind's eye. "Three!"

He pushed open the door, his body tingling. His limbs grew and morphed as the others ran past him. Their group rippled as they shifted from their chosen shapes and sizes into tall, slender aliens.

Adrian felt himself settle into his new form. He looked to Lola and Anna, who had both chosen Jack's cronies, Terin and Joro.

He had chosen Jack.

"Great minds," Lola said.

"Are you crazy?" Anna said, looking him up and down.

"It's my best bet."

"For what?"

"You'll see. Cover me?"

"Wait!" Lola grabbed Adrian's hand and pressed something into it. "The map."

"Thanks. Ready?"

She and Lola nodded and together they ran into the army of aliens. As Adrian had hoped, all of them looked around wildly at these new additions to their group. Within a minute, they had lowered their weapons, unsure whom to shoot.

Adrian looked around, trying to spot Jack, but she was nowhere to be found.

They reached the door to the lair, which he had only ever gotten through with Caesar chaperoning him.

"Now what?" Anna said.

"We need a robot to get in."

"Come on, Fiona," Lola muttered.

They watched the sky, lit up with red laser light, and circling drones. More rebels were surely dying inside. He just needed to get inside.

"What about the room with the pipes?" Adrian asked.

"They know that's the way we left," Anna said. "We don't know if it's compromised by now."

Adrian looked around at the robots mingling with the aliens. Not far off, he spotted Caesar. Of course, they had reactivated him.

"Follow my lead," he said and set off toward him. He adjusted his posture, lifting his chin and setting his shoulders back, doing his best impression of Jack.

"Caesar," he called to the robot. "Come."

Caesar swiveled and made his way over. "Warden. How can I be of service?"

Adrian's heart fell to his gut. How did he know it was him?

Anna and Lola looked at him in panic.

"I need to get inside," he tried.

"I am under strict orders not to allow you in. Especially after what you pulled last time."

"I'm sorry about that, Caesar. But the fate of the world is kind of in my hands right now."

"I'm sorry, warden. I must follow orders." The robot swiveled and lifted his metal arms to the sky. Suddenly all the drones froze in mid-trajectory and circled around into formation, heading right for them.

Lola pushed Anna and Adrian back, holding her gun at the ready. "I'll hold them off. Run!"

Before Adrian knew what was happening, Anna grabbed his arm and pulled him toward the lair once again. Whining light sounded dangerously close to their ears. Anna veered right and ducked behind a pile of fallen aliens. Adrian rolled to a stop beside her. There they heaved, catching their breaths as laser fire lit up the sky.

"What—now?" Adrian asked.

Anna shook her head as a laser beam shot above it.

Both of them flinched and sank lower.

"This is it," she panted. "All that work. All those years of planning. You were right all along, Adrian. We never had a chance of winning."

Adrian clutched her hand. "Don't say that. We're going to get through this."

"How do you know?"

"Because you were right. I always run away. I didn't want to see what was happening around me. If it wasn't for you and Lola and the rebel cause, none of us would've even made it this far. At least if we—" he almost couldn't say it. "If we die then we die together, fighting, knowing we did everything we could until the end."

Anna's eyes locked on his, her usual fiery gaze back. "We go out fighting." She stood and helped Adrian up.

"Till the end," he said.

Flashes of light shot all around them as they ran back toward the lair, where Lola was still shooting at the sky.

Suddenly, an eerie silence spread across the area. Every single drone stopped mid-hover and then fell to the ground with a clunk. Caesar, too, collapsed. As did every other robot among the aliens.

"Fiona!" Anna and Adrian said in unison.

Just in front of them, the lair's entrance sighed open.

Anna grabbed his hand again. "We'll do it together. Just like your parents."

Adrian's heart swelled. He nodded and they walked forward, every alien's eye set on them in confusion. Lola nodded curtly at them as they passed, her gun at the ready pointing down into the alien crowd. She wouldn't shoot, he knew. Not with her people spread throughout. But they didn't know that.

It was almost too easy now. Into the lair, they walked. Through the disabled decontamination chamber. Into the main lobby, lit red with backup lighting.

Adrian pulled out the digital map, which projected in front of them.

"This way," Anna said, heading down the first hallway.

They followed the map's navigation, turning when it said. Finally, they descended the stairs to the bottom floor—the same floor where the shifters had been experimented on.

It looked the same as when they had escaped through the trash chute. The halls blinked red, making it hard to see the doors lining the walls. They followed the map to the end of the hall, to an old elevator. Or what used to be an elevator. The elevator car had been removed so the shaft was empty. Something beneath it glowed. Adrian's skin perspired from the heat emanating from the space.

Adrian kept hold of Anna's hand as he leaned over to see what lay below. He had to shield his eyes from the blinding light.

"That's it. It's down there."

"Okay, let's do it," she said.

A voice echoed in the narrow space. "Well, well, well. We are clever, aren't we?"

Adrian and Anna turned. Jack walked gracefully from the other end of the hall, her two real cronies behind her, clutching a struggling Fiona between them.

22

"I SHOULD HAVE KNOWN she was working with you rebels," Jack said, her eyes flicking to the real Fiona.

"Leave her alone," Adrian said.

"So she can destroy more of my precious technology? To think I trusted her as my assistant." She signaled to her cronies and they tightened their grip on Fiona, pulling her into the closest room. Fiona let out a cry.

"Actually, that was me." Anna transformed in an instant into Fiona's double. "Now let her go."

If Jack was surprised, she didn't show it.

Adrian's heart quickened. "Don't, Anna," he hissed.

She looked from him to his watch and back again. Then she rushed forward, bowling Jack's cronies over so that she, the real Fiona, and the aliens were tangled in a confused heap.

Adrian seized the opportunity and activated the watch's mechanism that would disable the aliens' energy source.

"No!" Jack was beside him in an instant, her willowy arms around him, grasping for the watch.

"It's not what you think," Adrian grunted. "It's preventing you—"

"You'll kill us all." She wrestled him to the ground, surprisingly strong considering they were currently an equal match.

Adrian's only advantage was that the watch was still secured on his wrist.

Flashes of smoking laser light blasted around the narrow hallway, where shouts and cries echoed.

Adrian managed to flip over and glimpsed two limp forms against the wall. One of Jack's cronies. The other—one of the Fionas.

"Anna!" Adrian called, seeing the second Fiona roiling on the ground, clutching her side. The smell of burnt skin reached his nose.

"No!" Adrian struggled underneath Jack. "Enough killing. Enough fighting."

"Give me the watch," she whispered, "and all of this will be over."

"Don't do it," one of the Fionas gasped. "Finish—it—Adrian."

"You don't want this, Adrian," Jack said. "I knew from the moment I met you that you understood your place. You understood there is a greater good we're working for. That if everyone stays in line, then no one has to die. No one will want for anything. All you have to do is give me the watch. And everything will go back to the way it was."

The way it was.

A barrage of images flooded Adrian's mind. His parents kissing him goodbye the night they died. The police officers who woke him up to give him the watch as consolation. The raids on shapeshifters. Zeke's family taking him in. Bonding with Anna in secret. Anna's increasing secrecy as she attended more rebel rallies. Hiding his true form. The overcrowding prisons. The rebel underground. Blood Cry's training. Jack's experimentation rooms—all of it flashed at lightning speed.

Adrian didn't want things to go back to the way they were. The way it was wasn't working. For anyone. Not even Jack.

She continued talking, her voice growing more urgent. "If you do this, you're exterminating my race. You'll have the blood of my people on your hands. You don't want that."

"You're right," he managed. "We have to do what's best for the greater good." He yanked his arm from under her and pressed the button to open the watch.

Adrian felt the cold end of a laser gun press against the back of his ribcage. "I didn't want to do this, but you give me no choice. Now deactivate it."

Adrian froze, putting his hands flat to show surrender.

"Good," she said. "Now slowly, very slowly, take off the watch."

Adrian followed her instructions, moving extra slow. He unlatched the watch from his wrist, loosening it just enough to give him the extra room he needed.

He closed his eyes and thought of his parents, their images fresh from his time in the watch. His body tingled and warmth spread through him as he shifted into his true form.

The laser gun slid from his back as Jack lost balance on top of him.

Without thinking, he rolled over, sending Jack over the edge of the shaft.

He felt a tug on his tail, and suddenly he was sliding over the edge too.

All he could do was twist the final mechanism on the watch and point it down toward the energy source.

A blinding light overtook the shaft. And then everything went dark.

23

ADRIAN DIDN'T KNOW the moment he had stopped falling, but he had. Far below him was darkness. Jack's pitch black figure lay somewhere below, unmoving.

Something cut into Adrian's right side. He patted the area to feel an elevator cable wrapped tightly around his leg and tail. The cables had caught him. Saved him from meeting the same fate as Jack.

In his dragon form, he nearly filled out the elevator shaft. He twisted, attempting to untangle himself from the cord, but pain shot up his right side.

"Anna?" He called. And then, pit in his stomach, "Fiona?"

A body shuffled closer from above, slowly. Grunting. Adrian craned his neck to see the face that would appear above him.

"Adrian!"

It was Fiona's. Or at least what looked like hers.

"Hold on," she said, and swung her feet over the edge, pulling the upper end of the cables toward her.

It was not the time to ask who she was. Or the condition of the other person who hadn't come over to help.

With an extra pair of hands working the cables, they managed to untangle his leg and tail. Adrian used what strength he could to climb up the shaft as one of the Fionas hoisted him simultaneously.

Once he was out, both of them collapsed, panting on the hallway floor. Adrian glimpsed the other Fiona, still slumped against the wall. Unmoving.

"Is it—are you . . . ?"

"It's me, Adrian." And then, in an instant, Fiona transformed into a tiger—the Anna he knew and loved.

Adrian threw his arms around her, hugging her as if it was the last time he would ever see her. As if letting go would make her vanish forever.

"Did—did it work?" she asked into his shoulder.

"I think so." He held up his wrist, his father's watch resting there unassumingly, as if nothing had happened.

"I don't understand," Anna said. "How did you know . . . ?"

"My parents—the night they died they were on a mission. A mission Madame Universe sent them on."

"Wait. Madame Universe, like the fairytale?"

"The legend, but yes, that one. Before she could help destroy the energy source, she needed to understand what it was. Their mission was basically like uploading software on a computer so she could analyze it. To know what we were up against. They died to ensure the upload finished."

"But your dad had the watch on. How did they know it wouldn't be taken?"

"To everyone else, it was just a watch. Even Lola didn't know because it was too dangerous. I think she figured it out eventually, but realized it was my mission, not hers. She was right."

Anna pulled his hand to her eye level, gently twisting it to examine the watch. "All this time. Right under our noses."

"Under mine, technically." Adrian looked away. "If I had only figured it out sooner . . ." His gaze floated over her shoulder, to the real Fiona. His stomach twisted.

They helped each other stand and walked over to her. Adrian bent down beside her, catching a strand of her hair on his finger and pulling it away to reveal two peacefully shut eyelids.

"I already checked." Anna's voice caught.

Adrian nodded and looked around the desolate, cold hallway. Then he did what he hoped someone would do for him. He hoisted her onto his shoulder. "She deserves a proper burial."

Anna nodded, tears streaming down her face.

Once outside, Adrian gently placed Fiona's body on the ground. Lola and Blood Cry rushed over.

As both of them bent down to grieve Fiona, Adrian walked forward. A sea of aliens stood, confused and on guard. Half with guns, half wrestling with one another.

"Jack is dead," Adrian called. "The alien energy source is destroyed."

An anxious murmur ran through the crowd. A few of the aliens lifted their guns. Still, others clutched their necks and chests, as if at any moment they would self-implode.

Adrian put his hands up. "Before you go on shooting, take off your masks."

They exchanged looks, some defiant, some apprehensive.

Adrian tried again. "Shapeshifters. Return to your natural form. Let the others see you for who you really are."

A ripple ran through the crowd as, one by one, each person shifted. Dragons, dogs, horses, cats. Every color, shape, and size imaginable.

"I understand if you don't trust me," Adrian said. "Not long ago, I wouldn't have trusted you. We were divided. At the mercy of a power that never belonged here. A power that interfered with this planet's natural ability to harmonize the creatures who live on it. But your leader is gone. And I'm not standing here as your leader. I am standing here to tell you that you are free. All of you."

Lola, Anna, and Blood Cry came to stand beside him.

"Take off your masks or don't," he continued. "It's your choice. But either way, you are safe."

One of the aliens stepped forward. He hesitated, but then, in one swift motion, pulled the mask from his face. He stood still for a moment, holding his breath. And then opened his mouth.

He laughed. "I can breathe!"

Several others tore their masks off. Eventually, the air was filled with joyous laughter and shouting.

Adrian waited for the noise to subside. "As warden, I declare the prison permanently closed. We have a lot to rebuild. A lot to figure out. But we're on the same side now. So let's figure it out together."

The crowd cheered. Adrian and his friends watched as aliens, shifters, and hybrids alike hugged and mingled, even helped each other with the dead, lining the bodies up in neat rows until they could receive a proper burial.

"I'll be right back," Adrian muttered to the others, making his way through the crowd, to the outskirts of the prison. A lone figure lay abandoned among the debris of battle. Adrian lowered to his knees beside Zeke. His eyes were still open, causing his expression to look surprised. Adrian gently shut his lids. "You deserved so much more, my friend," he whispered. Then he scooped him into his arms and carried him over to the line of other bodies.

■ ■ ■

Adrian wandered through the pristine cemetery, cradling a bouquet of flowers in his arms. The newly constructed grave markers glistened in the afternoon sunlight, made up of some premium alloy mixture the aliens insisted upon using. Adrian had to admit, even a year later, they looked as new as the day they had been installed.

They had decided not to separate the aliens from the hybrids, but to bury them together, side by side. This made finding Zeke's grave like winding through a maze with no directions.

On his third loop around the main walkway, he finally found him. Adrian placed the flowers on the grass below the grave plaque and then knelt before it.

He cleared his throat. "Hi, friend. It's uh—it's been a while."

A gentle breeze rustled the flowers.

"I wish you were here to see all this. To see what you helped create. Because you know we couldn't have don't it without you—"

Adrian's voice cracked. He inhaled sharply and sat for a while silently.

"If I could do it all over again, rewind to the day the rebels enlisted me, I would tell you. Everything. Even if you said I was crazy or turned me in. I know you wouldn't have. If I had just clued you in sooner . . ."

He had had this one-sided conversation almost every day since the battle. Run through his head a million scenarios in which Zeke had not been shot. Had made it to the prison safely with everyone he rescued. But his dreams always showed him the truth. That he had led Zeke directly into a trap.

"I guess what I'm trying to say is I'm sorry," he continued.

"Mr. Walker," a mechanical voice behind him said. "You are running behind schedule."

Adrian turned to find Caesar standing stiffly on the pathway.

"I'll be there in a minute." Adrian turned back to Zeke's grave, tracing his fingers along his name.

"Mr. Walker. I have entered the logistics of your friend's death into my algorithm and out of one million possibilities, there are only ten in which he lived. That is a .001% chance of survival."

"But it's a chance," Adrian said, standing and brushing off his pants.

Caesar shrieked.

"What?" Adrian looked around, trying to find the source of upset.

"Stains. Stains on your newly dry-cleaned pants!"

Adrian looked down to see the still-wet grass stains. "Oops."

"There is a plan, Mr. Walker. A plan you have downloaded to me, might I add. And it's already off track. Eight minutes behind schedule and dirty pants!"

"Okay, okay, I'm coming."

Caesar seemed to relax.

Adrian followed the robot to the car where Anna was waiting in the driver's seat.

"Did you say hi for me?" she asked, taking his hand as he entered the car.

Adrian nodded, a lump forming in his throat.

Caesar bent his stiff body, falling forward into the back seat. "I'm stuck!" he said. "Cars are not in my programming."

"Geez, do you think we could program some chill into Caesar?"

Anna laughed, tugging Caesar's arm to pull him the rest of the way in.

A few minutes later, they pulled up to the prison gates. Or what used to be gates. Now they rested wide open, with several varieties of vines and flowers wrapped around the wrought iron. Today fairy lights intertwined with the flowers, creating a welcoming glow to the festival within.

Anna, Adrian, and Caesar exited the car and walked inside, where aliens and hybrids intermingled, drinking and eating multicultural delicacies. The gardens were in full bloom. The jail cells were barless, retrofitted with handcrafted doors made of all sorts of materials.

The bars had been collected and recreated into a giant sculpture that sat in the center of the community: an alien stood in the center of a group of hybrids, each with their hands on its shoulder. By now flowers had grown their way up the bars, filling out their shapes with shades of red, yellow, and purple.

In front of the sculpture was a platform. Lola stood, addressing the crowd with a drink in hand. "Thank you all for gathering tonight to honor what we have built together over the last year. I don't think any of us could have foreseen how to get here or what it would take. What it would cost us on both sides."

Many people in the crowd bent their heads. Anna squeezed Adrian's hand. He squeezed back.

"But now there are no sides. Just one unit. And looking back, I don't think I could have expected anything better to come out of this. So let's raise our glasses. To the fallen, to those who helped us get to this moment and who unfortunately cannot enjoy it, and most importantly, to each other. Here, together, now. Cheers."

The crowd raised their glasses in unison, a ripple of "cheers!" echoing out into the sunset.

Lola scanned the crowd, her eyes pausing on Adrian. She gave him a knowing look. He smiled, sending back an imperceptible nod.

"And now," Lola called over the noise—a skill she had only gotten better at. "I would like to invite up Adrian Walker, who has a few words he'd like to say."

The crowd murmured, looking around for Adrian.

Adrian loosened his grasp on Anna's hand. She looked sideways at him, eyebrows raised, and let his hand go.

All eyes were on Adrian as he walked up to that stage. His heart pounded worse than in all the life-or-death situations he had found himself in that past year. He patted his pocket, making sure the box was still there. It was.

"I'll keep this short," he said, "I couldn't think of a better time or place to do this. So . . ." He got down on one knee and extracted the box from his pocket. He searched the crowd for Anna, finding her exactly where he left her. "Anna, we've been through a lot together. At some points, I thought I'd lost you. At one point, I had convinced myself we weren't right for each other anymore. But this past year has shown me you have been there for me the whole time. That even when I wavered, when I changed my mind, when I felt lost, you were there, solid as ever. I never want to lose you again." He opened the box to reveal a brilliant crystal ring. "Will you marry me?"

Anna was already nodding, crying, making her way forward to the stage. Adrian stepped down and met her in the crowd, which was now going wild with cheers and shouts.

Adrian held the ring out to her and she offered her hand. He slipped it onto her finger. And she threw her arms around him and kissed him.

The crowd enveloped them, aliens and hybrids patting them on the back, hugging them, lifting them into the air, dancing around them. Adrian imagined his parents and Anna's parents in the crowd, celebrating along with them. They might not have been there to see it, but he knew they knew he had done it. After all these years their dream of a better world had come true.

The End—Or is it?

ACKNOWLEDGMENTS

I am grateful to many wonderful people who helped in the process of creating this book.

Most importantly, I thank my family for their support and encouragement: my mom for being with me for every step; my dad, brother, and cousin Alesse for reading drafts of the book and giving me their notes; my Tanta for reading drafts and giving me support throughout the process; and my cousin Melissa—this book wouldn't have happened without you.

Thank you to the talented Charlie Lively for bringing the story to life with your illustrations. Also to Jeniffer Thompson and her team at Monkey C. Media for making the publishing process fun and easy. And to Adrienne Moch for copyediting the book and Stephanie Thompson for proofreading it.

Thank you to Jenn Denham for the marketing and outreach associated with this book and me as an author.

I'd also like to give a special thanks to my family dogs, Lola, Leia, and Lily (RIP), for their constant emotional support.

ABOUT THE AUTHOR

DAVID DANN describes himself as "a simple man with simple needs." Diagnosed with verbal apraxia at the age of two and autism at the age of four, David had trouble expressing himself from a young age. Growing up, he found a deep connection to animals—especially his family dogs Lily, Lola, and Leia, who provided emotional support and ultimately the inspiration to  write this book. Reading and watching science fiction also helped David discover more about himself and his passion for storytelling. A San Diego native, David now lives in Montana, where there's plenty of room for more animals in his life. To learn more about David Dann and Hidden Shifters, visit DavidDannAuthor.com.

ABOUT THE ILLUSTRATOR

CHARLIE LIVELY is an artist who works in a variety of genres such as realism, cartoon art, traditional art, and graphic design. His passion for history and interest in the development of art over time informs his style and works. A San Diego native, his inspiration and drive comes from his maternal grandfather, who was a source of encouragement and motivation throughout childhood. Follow him on instagram @chucks_art04.